As for winning he...
his wife...

Trying to charm her into marrying him wasn't likely to work. Those blazing dark eyes of hers would shoot down every move he made in that direction. No way would she believe he cared about her. So what would work?

She had just offered him a deal.

Why not offer her one?

Make it a deal too attractive to refuse.

Initially a French/English teacher, **Emma Darcy** changed careers to computer programming before the happy demands of marriage and motherhood. Very much a people person, and always interested in relationships, she finds the world of romance fiction a thrilling one, and the challenge of creating her own cast of characters very addictive.

Recent titles by the same author:

THE COSTARELLA CONQUEST
HIDDEN MISTRESS, PUBLIC WIFE
THE BILLIONAIRE'S HOUSEKEEPER MISTRESS

Did you know these are also available as eBooks?
Visit www.millsandboon.co.uk

AN OFFER
SHE CAN'T REFUSE

BY
EMMA DARCY

MILLS & BOON

DID YOU PURCHASE THIS BOOK WITHOUT A COVER?

If you did, you should be aware it is **stolen property** as it was reported *unsold and destroyed* by a retailer. Neither the author nor the publisher has received any payment for this book.

All the characters in this book have no existence outside the imagination of the author, and have no relation whatsoever to anyone bearing the same name or names. They are not even distantly inspired by any individual known or unknown to the author, and all the incidents are pure invention.

All Rights Reserved including the right of reproduction in whole or in part in any form. This edition is published by arrangement with Harlequin Enterprises II BV/S.à.r.l. The text of this publication or any part thereof may not be reproduced or transmitted in any form or by any means, electronic or mechanical, including photocopying, recording, storage in an information retrieval system, or otherwise, without the written permission of the publisher.

This book is sold subject to the condition that it shall not, by way of trade or otherwise, be lent, resold, hired out or otherwise circulated without the prior consent of the publisher in any form of binding or cover other than that in which it is published and without a similar condition including this condition being imposed on the subsequent purchaser.

® and TM are trademarks owned and used by the trademark owner and/or its licensee. Trademarks marked with ® are registered with the United Kingdom Patent Office and/or the Office for Harmonisation in the Internal Market and in other countries.

First published in Great Britain 2012
by Mills & Boon, an imprint of Harlequin (UK) Limited.
Harlequin (UK) Limited, Eton House, 18-24 Paradise Road,
Richmond, Surrey TW9 1SR

© Emma Darcy 2012

ISBN: 978 0 263 89036 5

Harlequin (UK) policy is to use papers that are natural, renewable and recyclable products and made from wood grown in sustainable forests. The logging and manufacturing process conform to the legal environmental regulations of the country of origin.

Printed and bound in Spain
by Blackprint CPI, Barcelona

AN OFFER
SHE CAN'T REFUSE

CHAPTER ONE

'It's like a great big sail, Mama,' Theo said in awe, staring up at the most famous building in Dubai—Burj Al Arab, the only seven-star hotel in the world.

Tina Savalas smiled at her beautiful five-year-old son. 'Yes, it's meant to look like that.'

Built on a man-made island surrounded by the sea, the huge white glittering structure had all the glorious elegance of a sail billowed by the wind. Tina was looking forward to seeing as much of its interior as she could. Her sister, Cassandra, had declared it absolutely fabulous, a must-see on their two-day stopover before flying on to Athens.

Actually staying in the hotel was way too expensive—thousands of dollars a night—which was fine for the super-rich to whom the cost was totally irrelevant. People like Theo's father. No doubt *he* had occupied one of the luxury suites with butler on his way back to Greece from Australia, having put his *charming episode* with her behind him.

Tina shut down on the bitter thought. Being left pregnant by Ari Zavros was her own stupid fault. She'd been a completely blind naive fool to have believed he was as much in love with her as she was with him. Sheer fantasy land. Besides, how could she regret having Theo? He was the most adorable little boy, and from time to time, knowing Ari was missing out on his son gave her considerable secret satisfaction.

Their taxi stopped at the checkpoint gates which prevented anyone but paying guests from proceeding to the hotel. Her mother produced the necessary paperwork, showing confirmation that they had booked for the early afternoon tea session. Even that was costing them one hundred and seventy dollars each, but they had decided it was a once-in-a-lifetime experience they should indulge in.

The security man waved them on and the taxi drove slowly over the bridge which led to the hotel entrance, allowing them time to take in the whole amazing setting.

'Look, Mama, a camel!' Theo cried, delighted at recognising the animal standing on a side lawn.

'Yes, but not a real one, Theo. It's a statue.'

'Can I sit on it?'

'We'll ask if you can, but later, when we're leaving.'

'And take a photo of me on it so I can show my friends,' he pressed eagerly.

'I'm sure we'll have plenty of great photos to show from this trip,' Tina assured him.

They alighted from the taxi and were welcomed into the grand lobby of the hotel which was so incredibly opulent, photographs couldn't possibly capture all of its utter magnificence. They simply stood and stared upwards at the huge gold columns supporting the first few tiers of inner balconies of too many floors to count, the rows of their scalloped ceilings graduating from midnight-blue to aqua and green and gold at the top with lots of little spotlights embedded in them, twinkling like stars.

When they finally lowered their heads, right in front of them and dividing two sets of escalators, was a wonderful cascade of dancing fountains, each level repeating the same range of colours in the tower of ceilings. The escalators were flanked by side-walls which were gigantic aquariums where hosts of gorgeous tropical fish darted and glided around the underwater rocks and foliage.

'Oh, look at the fish, Mama!' Theo cried, instantly entranced by them.

'This truly is amazing,' Tina's mother murmured in awe. 'Your father always liked the architecture of the old world. He thought nothing could beat the palaces and the cathedrals that were built in the past, but this is absolutely splendid in its own way. I wish he was here to see it.'

He had died a year ago and her mother still wore black in mourning. Tina missed him, too. Despite his disappointment in her—getting pregnant to a man who was not interested in partnering her for life—he had given her the support she'd needed and been a marvellous grandfather to Theo, proud that she'd named her son after him.

It was a terrible shame that he hadn't lived long enough to see Cassandra married. Her older sister had done everything right; made a success of her modelling career without the slightest taint of scandal in her private life, fell in love with a Greek photographer—the *right* nationality—who wanted their wedding to take place on Santorini, the most romantic Greek island of all. He would have been bursting with pride, walking Cassandra down the aisle next week, his *good* girl.

But at least the *bad* girl had given him the pleasure of having a little boy in the family. Having only two daughters and no son had been another disappointment to her father. Tina told herself she had made up for her *mistake* with Theo. And she'd been on hand to take over the management of his restaurant, doing everything *his* way when he'd become too ill to do it all himself. He'd called her a *good girl* then.

Yet while Tina thought she had redeemed herself in her father's eyes, she didn't feel good inside. Not since Ari Zavros had taken all that she was and walked away from her as though she was nothing. The sense of being totally crushed had never gone away. Theo held her together. He made life worth living. And there were things to enjoy, like this hotel with all its splendours.

There was another glorious fountain at the top of the escalator. They were escorted down a corridor to the elevator which would whiz them up to the SkyView Bar on the twenty-seventh floor. They walked over a large circle of mosaic tiles, a blazing sun at its centre, over a carpet shaped like a fish in red and gold. Her mother pointed out vases of tightly clustered red roses, dozens of them in each perfect pompom-like arrangement. The

doors of the elevator were patterned in blue and gold—
everything unbelievably rich.

On arriving in the shimmering gold lobby of the bar,
they were welcomed again and escorted into the dining
area where the decor was a stunning blue and green,
the ceiling designed like waves with white crests. They
were seated in comfortable armchairs at a table by a
window which gave a fantastic view of the city of Dubai
and the man-made island of Palm Jumeirah where the
very wealthy owned mansions with sand and sea front-
age.

A whole world away from her life in every sense,
Tina thought, but she was having a little taste of it today,
smiling at the waiter who handed them a menu listing
dozens of varieties of tea from which they could choose,
as many different ones as they liked to try throughout
the afternoon. He poured them glasses of champagne to
go with their first course which was a mix of fresh ber-
ries with cream. Tina didn't know how she was going
to get through all the marvellous food listed—probably
not—but she was determined on enjoying all she could.

Her mother was smiling.

Theo was wide-eyed at the view.

This was a good day.

Ari Zavros was bored. It had been a mistake to invite Felicity Fullbright on this trip to Dubai with him,
though it had certainly proved he couldn't bear to have
her as a full-time partner. She had a habit of notching
up experiences as though she had a bucket list that had

to be filled. Like having to do afternoon tea at the Burj Al Arab hotel.

'I've done afternoon tea at The Ritz and The Dorchester in London, at the Waldorf Astoria in New York, and at The Empress on Vancouver Island. I can't miss out on this one, Ari,' she had insisted. 'The sheikhs are mostly educated in England, aren't they? They probably do it better than the English.'

No relaxing in between his business talks on the Palm Jumeirah development. They had to visit the indoor ski slope, Atlantis underwater, and of course the gold souks where she had clearly expected him to buy her whatever she fancied. She was not content with just his company and he was sick to death of hers.

The only bright side of Felicity Fullbright was she did shut up in bed where she used her mouth in many pleasurable ways. Which had swayed him into asking her to accompany him on this trip. However, the hope that she might be compatible with him on other grounds was now comprehensively smashed. The good did not balance out the bad and he'd be glad to be rid of her tomorrow.

Once they flew into Athens he would pack her off back to London. No way was he going to invite her to his cousin's wedding on Santorini. His father could rant and rave as much as he liked about its being time for Ari to shed his bachelor life. Marriage to the Fullbright heiress was not going to happen.

There had to be someone somewhere he could tolerate as his wife. He just had to keep looking and assessing whether a marriage would work well enough. His father was right. It *was* time to start his own family. He did want children, always enjoying the time he spent with his nephews. However, finding the right woman to partner him in parenthood was not proving easy.

Being head over heels in love like his cousin, George, was not a requirement. In fact, having been scorched by totally mindless passion in his youth, Ari had never wanted to feel so *possessed* by a woman again. He had a cast-iron shield up against being sucked into any blindly driven emotional involvement. A relationship either satisfied him on enough levels to be happily viable or it didn't—a matter of completely rational judgement.

His *dissatisfaction* with Felicity was growing by the minute. Right now she was testing his patience, taking millions of photographs of the inside of the hotel. It wasn't enough to simply look and enjoy, share the visual pleasure of it with him. Using the camera to the nth degree was more important, taking pictures that she would sift through endlessly and discard most of them. Another habit he hated. He liked to live in the moment.

Finally, *finally,* they got in the elevator and within minutes were being led to their window table in the SkyView Bar. But did Felicity sit down and enjoy the view? No, the situation wasn't perfect for her.

'Ari, I don't like this table,' she whispered, grasping his arm to stop him from sitting down.

'What's wrong with it?' he asked tersely, barely containing his exasperation with her constant self-centred demands.

She nodded and rolled her eyes, indicating the next

table along. 'I don't want to be next to a child. He'll probably play up and spoil our time here.'

Ari looked at the small family group that Felicity didn't like. A young boy—five or six years old—stood at the window, staring down at the wave-shaped Jumeirah Beach Hotel. Seated beside the child on one side was a very handsome woman—marvellous facial bones like Sophia Loren's—dark wavy hair unashamedly going grey, probably the boy's grandmother. On the other side with her back turned to him was another woman, black hair cropped short in a modern style, undoubtedly younger, a slimmer figure, and almost certainly the boy's mother.

'He won't spoil the food or the tea, Felicity, and if you haven't noticed, all the other tables are taken.'

They'd been late arriving, even later because of feeding her camera in the lobby. Having to wait for Felicity to be satisfied with whatever she wanted was testing his temper to an almost intolerable level.

She placed a pleading hand on his arm, her big blue eyes promising a reward if he indulged her. 'But I'm sure if you ask, something better could be arranged.'

'I won't put other people out,' he said, giving her a hard, quelling look. 'Just sit down, Felicity. Enjoy being here.'

She pouted, sighed, flicked her long blonde hair over her shoulder in annoyance, and finally sat.

The waiter poured them champagne, handed them menus, chatted briefly about what was on offer, then quickly left them before Felicity could kick up another fuss which would put him in a difficult position.

'Why do they have all those chairs on the beach set out in rows, Yiayia?'

The boy's voice was high and clear and carried, bringing an instant grimace to Felicity's pouty mouth. Ari recognised the accent as Australian, yet the boy had used the Greek word for grandmother, arousing his curiosity.

'The beach belongs to the hotel, Theo, and the chairs are set out for the guests so they will be comfortable,' the older woman answered, her English thick with a Greek accent.

'They don't do that at Bondi,' the boy remarked.

'No. That's because Bondi is a public beach for anyone to use and set up however they like on the sand.'

The boy turned to her, frowning at the explanation. 'Do you mean I couldn't go to that beach down there, Yiayia?'

He was a fine-looking boy, very pleasing features and fairish hair. Oddly enough he reminded Ari of himself as a child.

'Not unless you were staying in the hotel, Theo,' his grandmother replied.

'Then I think Bondi is better,' the boy said conclusively, turning back to the view.

An egalitarian Australian even at this tender age, Ari thought, remembering his own experiences of the people's attitudes in that country.

Felicity huffed and whined, 'We're going to have to listen to his prattle all afternoon. I don't know why people bring children to places like this. They should be left with nannies.'

'Don't you like children, Felicity?' Ari enquired, hoping she would say no, which would comprehensively wipe out any argument his father might give him over his rejection of this marital candidate.

'In their place,' she snapped back at him.

Out of sight, out of mind, was what she meant.

'I think family is important,' he drawled. 'And I have no objection to any family spending time together, anywhere.'

Which shut her up, temporarily.

This was going to be a *long* afternoon.

Tina felt the nape of her neck prickling at the sound of the man's voice coming from the table next to theirs. The deep mellifluous tone was an electric reminder of another voice that had seduced her into believing all the sweet things it had said to her, believing they had meant she was more special than any other woman in the world.

It couldn't be Ari, could it?

She was torn by the temptation to look.

Which was utterly, utterly stupid, letting thoughts of him take over her mind when she should be enjoying this wonderfully decadent afternoon tea.

Ari Zavros was out of her life. Well and truly out of it. Six years ago he'd made the parting from her absolutely decisive, no coming back to Australia, no interest in some future contact. She had been relegated to *a fond memory,* and she certainly didn't want *the fond memory* revived here and now, if by some rotten coincidence it was Ari sitting behind her.

It wouldn't be him, anyway.

The odds against it were astronomical.

All the same, it was better not to look, better to keep her back turned to the man behind her. If it was Ari, if he caught her looking and recognised her...it was a stomach-curdling thought. No way was she prepared for a face-to-face meeting with him, especially not with her mother and Theo looking on, becoming involved.

This couldn't happen.

It wouldn't happen.

Her imagination was making mountains out of no more than a tone of voice. Ridiculous! The man was with a woman. She'd heard the plummy English voice complaining about Theo's presence—a really petty complaint because Theo was always well-behaved. She shouldn't waste any attention on them. Her mind fiercely dictated ignoring the couple and concentrating on the pleasure of being here.

She leaned forward, picked up her cup and sipped the wonderfully fragrant *Jasmin Pearls*. They had already eaten a marvellous slice of Beef Wellington served warm with a beetroot puree. On their table now was a stand shaped like the Burj, its four tiers presenting a yummy selection of food on colourful glass plates.

At the top were small sandwiches made with different types of bread—egg, smoked salmon, cream cheese with sun-dried tomatoes, cucumber and cream cheese. Other tiers offered seafood vol-au-vents with prawns, choux pastry chicken with seeded mustard, a beef sandwich, and basil, tomato and bocconcini cheese on squid ink bread. It was impossible to eat everything. Predictably,

Theo zeroed in on the chicken, her mother anything with cheese, and the seafood she loved was all hers.

A waiter came around with a tray offering replenishments but they shook their heads, knowing there was so much more to taste—fruit cake, scones with and without raisins and an assortment of spreads; strawberry and rose petal jam, clotted cream, a strawberry mousse and tangy passionfruit.

Tina refused to let the reminder of Ari Zavros ruin her appetite. There wasn't much conversation going on at the table behind her anyway. Mostly it was the woman talking, carrying on in a snobby way, comparing this afternoon tea to others she'd had in famous hotels. Only the occasional murmur of reply came from the man.

'I'm so glad we stopped in Dubai,' her mother remarked, gazing at the view. 'There's so much amazing, creative architecture in this city. That hotel shaped like a wave just below us, the stunning buildings we passed on the way here. And to think it's all happened in the space of what…thirty years?'

'Something like that,' Tina murmured.

'It shows what can be done in these modern times.'

'With the money to do it,' Tina dryly reminded her.

'Well, at least they have the money. They're not bankrupting the country like the aristocrats did in Europe for their grand palaces in the old days. And all this has to be a drawcard for tourists, bringing money into the country.'

'True.' Tina smiled. 'I'm glad we came here, too. It certainly is amazing.'

Her mother leaned forward and whispered, 'Seated at the next table is an incredibly handsome man. I think he must be a movie star. Take a look, Tina, and see if you recognise him.'

Her stomach instantly cramped. Ari Zavros was an incredibly handsome man. Her mother nodded encouragingly, expecting her to glance around. Hadn't she already decided it couldn't—wouldn't—be him? One quick look would clear this silly fear. *Just do it. Get it over with.*

One quick look...

The shock of seeing the man she'd never expected to see again hit her so hard she barely found wits enough to give her mother a reply.

'I've never seen him in a movie.'

And thank God the turning of her head towards him hadn't caught his attention!

Ari!—still a beautiful lion of a man with his thick mane of wavy honey-brown hair streaked through with golden strands, silky smooth olive skin, his strongly masculine face softened by a beautifully sculptured full-lipped mouth, and made compelling by thickly lashed amber eyes—eyes that Theo had inherited, and thank God her mother hadn't noticed that likeness!

'Well, he must be *someone*,' her mother said in bemusement. 'One of the beautiful people.'

'Don't keep staring at him, Mama,' Tina hissed, everything within her recoiling from any connection with him.

Her mother was totally unabashed. 'I'm just returning the curiosity. He keeps looking at us.'

Why??? screamed through Tina's mind.

Panicky thoughts followed.

Had the Australian accent reminded him of the three months he'd spent there?

He could not have identified her, not from a back view. Her hair had been long and curly when he'd known her.

Did he see a similarity to himself in Theo?

But surely he wouldn't be making a blood connection to himself personally, unless he was in the habit of leaving love-children around the world.

Tina pulled herself up on that dark thought. He had used condoms with her. It was unlikely he would think his safe sex had ever been unsafe. Whatever had drawn his interest…it presented a very real problem to her.

Since he and his companion had arrived late at this afternoon tea, it was almost inevitable that she and Theo and her mother would leave before them and they would have to pass his table on their way out. If he looked straight at her, face-to-face…

He might not remember her. It had been six years ago. She looked different with her hair short. And he'd surely had many women pass through his life in the meantime. But if he did recognise her and stopped her from making a quick escape, forcing a re-acquaintance, introductions…her mind reeled away from all the painful complications that might follow.

She did not want Ari Zavros directly touching her life again. That decision had been made before her pregnancy had to be revealed to her parents. It would have been unbearable to have him questioning an unwelcome paternity or sharing responsibility for Theo on some dutiful basis—constantly in and out of her life, always making her feel bad for having loved him so blindly.

It had been a wretched business, standing firm

against her father's questioning, refusing to track down a man who didn't want her any more, insisting that her child would be better off without any interference from him. Whether that decision had been right or wrong she had never regretted it.

Even recently when Theo had asked why he didn't have a father like his kindergarten friends, she had felt no guilt at telling him that some children only had mothers and that was the way it was for them. She was convinced that Ari could only be a horribly disruptive influence in their lives if, given the chance, he decided to be in them at all.

She didn't want to give him the chance.

It had taken so much determination and hard work to establish the life she and Theo now had, it was imperative to hold onto the status quo. This terrible trick of fate—putting Ari and herself in the same place at the same time with Theo and her mother present—could mess up their lives so badly.

A confrontation *had* to be avoided.

Tina pushed back the sickening waves of panic and fiercely told herself this shouldn't be too difficult. Ari had company. Surely it would be unreasonable of him to leave his tete-a-tete with one woman to re-connect with another. Besides, he might not recognise her anyway. If he did, if he tried to engage her in some awful memory-lane chat, she had to ensure that her mother had already taken herself and Theo out of this possible scenario.

She could manage that.

She had to.

CHAPTER TWO

THE rest of afternoon tea took on a nightmarish quality for Tina. It was difficult to focus on the delicacies they were served, even more difficult to appreciate the marvellous range of tastes. Her mind was in a hopelessly scattered state. She felt like Alice in Wonderland at the mad hatter's tea party, with the red queen about to pounce and cut off her head.

Her mother demolished the fig tart and green-tea macaroon. Theo gobbled up the white chocolate cake. She forced herself to eat a caramel slice. They were then presented with another plate of wicked temptations: a strawberry dipped in white chocolate and decorated with a gold leaf, a meringue lemon tart, a passionfruit ball with an oozing liquid centre…more, more, more, and she had to pretend to enjoy it all while her stomach was in knots over Ari's presence behind her.

She smiled at Theo. She smiled at her mother. Her face ached with the effort to keep smiling. She silently cursed Ari Zavros for spoiling what should have been a special experience. The fear that he could spoil a lot more kept jogging through her mind. Finally her mother

called enough and suggested they return to the grand
lobby and take another leisurely look at everything before leaving.

'Yes, I want to see the fish again, Yiayia,' Theo
agreed enthusiastically. 'And sit on the camel.'

Tina knew this was the moment when she had to take
control. Every nerve in her body twanged at the vital
importance of it. She had already planned what to say.
It had to come out naturally, sound sensible. She forced
her voice to deliver what was needed.

'I think a toilet visit first might be a good idea. Will
you take Theo, Mama? I want to get a few photographs
from different windows up here. I'll meet you at the elevator.'

'Of course I'll take him. Come, Theo.'

She stood up and took his hand and they went off
happily together. Mission accomplished, Tina thought
on a huge wave of relief. Now, if she could get past Ari
without him taking any notice of her she was home free.
If the worst happened and he chose to intercept her de-
parture, she could deal with the situation on her own.

Having slung her travel bag over her shoulder, she
picked up her camera, stood at the window, clicked off
a few shots of the view, then, with her heart hammer-
ing, she turned, meaning to walk as quickly as she could
past the danger table.

Ari Zavros was looking straight at her. She saw the
jolt of recognition in his face, felt a jolt of shock run
right through her, rooting her feet to the floor, leaving
her standing like a mesmerised rabbit caught in head-
lights.

'Christina…' He spoke her name in a tone of pleasurable surprise, rising from his chair, obviously intent on renewing his *fond memory* of her.

No chance of escape from it. Her feet weren't receiving any messages from her brain which was totally jammed with all the misery this man had given her.

He excused himself from his companion who turned in her chair to give Tina a miffed look—long, silky, blonde hair, big blue eyes, peaches and cream complexion, definitely one of the beautiful people. Another *fond memory* for him, or something more serious this time?

It didn't matter. The only thing that mattered was getting this totally unwelcome encounter over and done with. Ari was approaching her, hands outstretched in charming appeal, his mouth tilting in a wry little smile.

'You've cut your beautiful hair,' he said as though that was a wicked shame.

Never mind the shame he'd left her in.

Her tongue leapt into life. 'I like it better short,' she said tersely, hating the reminder of how he'd enjoyed playing with the long curly tresses, winding it around his fingers, stroking it, kissing it, smelling it.

'What are you doing in Dubai?' he asked, his amber eyes twinkling with interest.

'Having a look at it. Why are you here?' she returned.

He shrugged. 'Business.'

'Mixed with pleasure,' she said dryly, with a nod at the blonde. 'Please…don't let me keep you from her, Ari. After all this time, what is there to say?'

'Only that it feels good to see you again. Even with

your cropped hair,' he replied with one of his megawatt smiles which had once melted her knees.

They stiffened in sheer rebellion. How dared he flirt with her when he was obviously connected to another woman? How dared he flirt with her at all when he'd used her up and left her behind him?

And she hated him saying it felt good to see her again when it made her feel so bad. He had no idea of what he'd done to her and she hated him for that, too. She wanted to smack that smile off his face, wanted to smack him down for having the arrogance to even approach her again with his smarmy charm, but the more dignified course, the *safer* course was simply to dismiss him.

'I'm a different person now to the one you knew,' she said oddly. 'If you'll excuse me, I'm with my mother who'll be waiting for me to catch up with her.'

Her feet obeyed the command to side-step, get moving To her intense frustration, Ari shot out a hand, clutching her arm, halting a swift escape from him. She glared at him, resentment burning deep from the touch of his fingers on her skin, from the power he still had to affect her physically. He was so close she could smell the cologne he used. It made her head swim with memories she didn't want to have.

The amber eyes quizzed hers, as though he didn't understand her cutting him off so abruptly. He wanted to know more. Never mind what she wanted.

'Your mother. And the boy...' he said slowly, obviously considering her family group and what it might mean.'You're married now? He is your son?'

Tina seethed. That, of course, would be so nice and neat, dismissing the intimacy they had shared as nothing important in her life, just as it hadn't been important to him.

She should say *yes*, have done with it. Let him think she was married and there was no possible place for him in her life. He would shut the door on his *charming episode* with her and let her go. She would be free of him forever.

Do it, do it! her mind screamed.

But her heart was being ripped apart by a violent tumult of emotions.

Another voice in her head was yelling *smack him with the truth!*

This man was Theo's father. She could not bring herself to palm his fatherhood off on anyone else. *He* ought to be faced with it. A savage recklessness streaked through her, obliterating any caring over what might happen next.

'I'm not married,' she slung at him. 'And yes, Theo is my son.'

He frowned.

Single motherhood did not sit so well with him. She was free but not free, tied to a child.

No ties for Ari Zavros.

That thought enraged Tina further. She fired bitter truth straight at him.

'He's also your son.'

It stunned him.

Totally stunned him.

No seductive smile.

No twinkly interest.

Blank shock.

With a sense of fiercely primitive satisfaction, Tina got her feet moving and strode past him, heading for the elevator where she hoped her mother and Theo would be waiting for her. She didn't think Ari would follow her. Not only had she cut his feet out from under him, but he was with another woman and it was highly unlikely that he'd want to face her with the complication of an illegitimate son.

Though a fast getaway from this hotel was definitely needed. No loitering in the lobby. She'd tell her mother she didn't feel well—too much rich food. It was true enough anyway. Her stomach was churning and she felt like throwing up.

She shouldn't have told Ari he was Theo's father. She hadn't counted on how much he could still get to her—his eyes, his touch, the whole insidious charisma of his close presence. Hopefully telling his wouldn't make any difference. For a start, he wouldn't want to believe her. Men like him usually denied paternity claims. Not that she would ever make any official claim on him. All the same, it had been stupid of her to throw the truth in his face and give herself this panic attack, stupid and reckless to have opened a door for him into her life again when she wanted him out, out, out!

Please, God, let him not follow up on it.

Let him shrug it off as a put-down line.

Let him just go on with his life and leave her alone to go on with hers.

That boy…his son? *His* son?

Ari snapped out of the wave of shock rolling through

his mind, swung on his heel, and stared after the woman who had just declared herself the mother of his child. Christina Savalas wasn't waiting around to capitalise on her claim. Having delivered her bombshell she was fast making an exit from any fall-out.

Was it true?

He quickly calculated precisely *when* he had been in Australia. It was six years ago. The boy's age would approximately fit that time-frame. He needed to know the actual birth date to be sure if it was possible. That could be checked. The name was Theo. Theo Savalas. Who looked very like himself as a child!

A chill ran down Ari's spine. If Theo was his, it meant he had left Christina pregnant, abandoned a pregnant woman, left her to bring up his child alone. But how could that happen when he was always careful to sheath himself against such a consequence? Not once had he ever failed to use protection. Had there been a slip-up with her, one that he didn't remember?

He did remember she'd been an innocent. Unexpectedly and delightfully so. He hadn't felt guilty about taking her virginity. Desire had been mutual and he'd given her pleasure—a good start to her sexual life, which he'd reasoned would become quite active as time went by. Any man would see her as desirable and it was only natural that she would be attracted to some of them.

But if he had left her pregnant... That would have messed up her career, messed up her life—reason enough for those extremely expressive dark eyes of hers to shoot black bolts of hatred and contempt at him with her punishing exit line.

Impossible to ignore what she'd said. He had to check it out. If the boy was his son... Why hadn't Christina told him about his existence before this? Why go it alone all these years? Why hit him with it now? There was a hell of a lot of questions to be considered.

'Ari...'

His teeth automatically gritted. He hated that whiny tone in Felicity's voice.

'What are you standing there for? She's gone.'

Gone but not forgotten.

'I was remembering my time in Australia, which was where I'd met Christina,' he said, forcing himself to return to his chair and be reasonably civil to the woman he had invited to be his companion.

'What were you doing in Australia?'

'Checking out the wine industry there. Seeing if any improvements could be made to the Santorini operation.'

'Was this Christina connected to the wine industry?'

The tone had changed to a snipe.

He shrugged. 'Not really. She was part of an advertising drive for the Jacob's Creek label.'

One eyebrow arched in knowing mockery. 'A model.'

'She was then.'

'And you had fun with her.'

He grimaced at her dig, which he found extremely distasteful in the circumstances. 'Ancient history, Felicity. I was simply surprised to see her here in Dubai.'

'Well, she's loaded down with a child now,' she said with snide satisfaction. 'No fun at all.'

'I can't imagine it is much fun, being a single mother,' he said, barely containing a wave of anger at Felicity's opinion.

'Oh, I don't know. Quite a few movie stars have chosen that route and they seem to revel in it.'

Ari wanted this conversation finished. He heaved a sigh, then mockingly drawled, 'What do I know? I'm a man.'

Felicity laughed, leaned over and stroked his thigh. 'And a gorgeous one, darling. Which is why I don't like you straying, even for a minute.'

The urge to stray to Christina Savalas had been instant.

He'd had his surfeit of self-centred women like Felicity Fullbright and the flash of memory—a sweet, charming time—had compelled him out of his seat. But it wasn't the same Christina he'd known. How could it be, given the passage of years? A different person, she'd said. He would need to get to know her again if she was the mother of his child.

He would track her down in the very near future. Obviously she was on a tourist trip with her mother and would be on the move for a few weeks. Best to wait until she was back on home ground. In the meantime, he had to sever any further involvement with Felicity, attend his cousin's wedding, then free himself up to pursue the big question.

Was Theo Savalas his son?

If the answer was a definitive yes, changes to his life had to be made.

And Christina Savalas would have to come to some accommodation with him, whether she liked it or not.

A father had rights to his child, and Ari had no qualms about enforcing them.

Family was family.

CHAPTER THREE

TINA felt continually tense for the rest of their short stay in Dubai, knowing Ari Zavros was in the same city. Although she didn't think he would pursue the paternity issue, and a second accidental encounter with him was unlikely, she only felt safe on the red tour bus in between its stops at the various points of interest; the gold souks, the spice markets, the shopping centres. It was a huge relief to board their flight to Athens on the third day, not having had any further contact with him.

They were met at the airport by Uncle Dimitri, her father's older brother. After a brief stop to check in at their hotel, he took them on to his restaurant which was sited just below the Acropolis and where all their Greek relatives had gathered to welcome them home. It wasn't home to Tina or Theo, both of whom had been born in Australia, but it was interesting to meet her mother's and father's families and it was a very festive get-together.

Her mother revelled in the company and Theo was a hit—*such a beautiful grandchild*—but Tina couldn't help feeling like an outsider. The women tended to talk about her in the third person, as though she wasn't there at all.

'We must find a husband for your daughter, Helen.'

'Why did she cut her hair? Men like long hair.'

'She is obviously a good mother. That is important.'

'And if she is used to helping in a restaurant…'

Not helping, *managing,* Tina silently corrected, observing how Uncle Dimitri was managing his. He was constantly on watch, signalling waiters to wherever service was required. All the patrons were treated to a plate of sliced watermelon at the end of their meals—on the house—a nice touch for long hot evenings. People left happy, which meant return visits and good word-of-mouth. It was something she could copy at home.

Most of the tables were out on the sidewalk, under trees or umbrellas. Herbs were grown in pots, their aromas adding to the pleasant ambience. The food was relatively simple, the salads very good. She particularly liked the olive oil, honey and balsamic vinegar dressing—a combination she would use in future. It was easy to relax and have a taste of Athens.

There'd been a message from Cassandra at the hotel, saying she and her fiancé would join them at the restaurant, and Tina kept looking for their arrival, eager to meet up with her sister again. Cass had brought George home to Sydney with her six months ago, but had been working a heavy international schedule ever since. They had just flown in from London and were spending one night in Athens before moving on to the island of Patmos where George's family lived.

'Here they come!' her mother cried, seeing them first.

Tina looked.

And froze in horror.

There was her beautiful sister, her face aglow with happy excitement, looking every inch the supermodel she had become.

Hugging her to his side was George Carasso, grinning with pride in his bride-to-be.

Next to him strolled Ari Zavros.

Her mother turned to her. 'Tina, isn't that the man we saw…'

She heard the words but couldn't answer. Bad enough to find herself confronted by him again. It was much, much worse with him knowing about Theo!

People were on their feet, greeting, welcoming, hugging and kissing. Ari was introduced as George's cousin who was to be his best man at the wedding. *His best man!* And she was Cass's only bridesmaid! The nightmare she had made for herself was getting more torturous by the second and there was no end to it any time soon. It was going to be impossible to enjoy her sister's wedding. She would have to suffer through being Ari's partner at the ceremony and the reception.

If she hadn't opened her mouth in Dubai and let her secret out, she might have managed to skate over their past involvement. There was little hope of that now. No hope at all, given the look Ari Zavros had just turned her way, a dangerously simmering challenge in the riveting amber eyes.

'And this is your sister?' he prompted Cass, who immediately obliged with the formal introduction.

'Yes. Tina! Oh, it's so good to see you again!' she bubbled, dodging around the table to give her a hug. 'George and I are staying in Ari's apartment tonight and when we told him we were meeting up with you, he insisted on coming with us so you won't be strangers to each other at the wedding.'

Strangers!

He hadn't let the cat out of the bag.

Tina fiercely hoped it suited him not to.

Cass swooped on Theo, lifting him up in her arms and turning to show him off to Ari. 'And this is my nephew, Theo, who is going to be our page boy.'

Ari smiled at him. 'Your Aunty Cassandra told me it's your birthday this week.'

He'd been checking, Tina thought grimly.

Theo held up his hand with fingers and thumb spread. 'Five,' he announced proudly.

'It's my birthday this month, too,' Ari said. 'That makes us both Leos.'

'No. I'm Theo, not Leo.'

Everyone laughed at the correction.

'He didn't mean to get your name wrong, darling,' Cass explained. 'We're all born under star signs and the star sign for your birthday is Leo. Which means a lion. And you have amber eyes, just like a lion.'

Theo pointed to Ari. 'He's got the same colour eyes as me.'

Tina held her breath. Her heart was drumming in her ears. Her mind was screaming *please, please, please don't claim parentage now.* It was the wrong place, the wrong time, the wrong everything!

'There you are, then,' Ari said with an air of indulgence, taking Theo's outstretched hand and giving it a light shake. 'Both of us are lions and I'm very glad to meet you.' He turned to Tina. 'And your mother.'

Relief reduced her to jelly inside. He wasn't pushing his fatherhood yet. Maybe he never would. She should be saying *hello,* but she was so choked up with nervous tension it was impossible to get her voice to work.

'Tina?' He gave her a slightly quizzical smile as he offered his hand to her. 'Short for Christina?'

'Yes.' It was a husky whisper, all she could manage.

Then she was forced by the occasion to let his strong fingers close around hers. The jolting sensation of electric warmth was a searing reminder of the sexual chemistry that had seduced her in the past. It instantly stirred a fierce rebellion in her mind. No way was she going to let it get to her again, making her weak and foolish. If there was to be a fight over custody of Theo, she couldn't let Ari Zavros have any personal power over her. She wriggled her hand out of his as fast as she could.

Seating was quickly re-arranged so that Cass and George could sit beside her mother. Uncle Dimitri produced an extra chair for Ari at the end of the table, right next to her and Theo. It was impossible for Tina to protest this proximity, given they would be partners at the wedding and apparently Ari had already stated his intention to *make her acquaintance.*

The situation demanded polite conversation. Any

failure to follow that course would raise questions about her behaviour. As much as Tina hated having to do it, she adopted the pretence of being strangers, forcing herself to speak to George's *best* man with an air of natural enquiry.

'When did you meet my sister?'

It was a good question. She needed information and needed it fast to help her deal with Ari in the most sensible way. If it was possible to avoid a showdown with him over Theo, grasping that possibility was paramount.

'Only this evening,' he answered with a wry little smile. 'I knew of her, of course, because of her engagement to George, but within the family she was always referred to as simply Cassandra since she is famously known by that name in the supermodel world. I'd never actually heard her surname. I chanced to see it written on her luggage when she set it down in the apartment. Very opportune, given the circumstances.'

The fact that he'd immediately seized the opportunity for a face-to-face meeting with her gave no support to the wishful thought of avoiding an ultimate showdown.

'So you proceeded to draw her out about her family,' Tina said flatly, feeling as though a trap was closing around her.

'Very enlightening,' he drawled, his eyes mocking the secrecy which was no longer a secret to him.

Fear squeezed her heart. Sheer self-defence demanded she ignore his enlightenment. 'You live in Athens?'

'Not really. The apartment is for convenience. Anyone in the family can use it, which is why George felt free to bring Cassandra there for tonight. More private for her than a hotel.'

'Very considerate of him,' she dryly remarked. 'Where do you normally live then?'

All she'd previously known about him was he belonged to a wealthy Greek family with an involvement in the wine industry. During the time they'd spent together, Ari had been more interested in everything Australian than talking about himself.

He shrugged. 'Various business interests require quite a bit of travelling but my family home is on Santorini.'

'We're going to Santorini,' Theo piped up, looked at Ari as though he was fascinated by the man.

Ari smiled at him. 'Yes, I know. Perhaps we could do something special together on your birthday.'

Tina's stomach contracted. He was intent on moving in on her, getting closer to their son.

'Like what?' Theo asked eagerly.

'Let's wait and see what we might like to do, Theo,' Tina cut in firmly, inwardly panicking at spending any more time than she absolutely had to with Ari Zavros. She didn't know if it was curiosity driving him or he was dabbling with the idea of claiming Theo as his flesh and blood. She turned hard, quelling eyes to him. 'You said *family home*. Does that mean you're married with children?'

He shook his head and made an ironic grimace. 'Much to my father's vexation, I am still single. It's his home I was referring to.'

'Not exactly single, Ari,' she tersely reminded him.

He knew she'd seen him with a woman in Dubai. She didn't have to spell that out. If he thought he could start playing fast and loose with her again, cheating on the beautiful blonde, he was on an ego trip she would take great satisfaction in smashing.

'I assure you I am, Christina,' he replied without the blink of an eyelid.

Her teeth gnashed over the lilted use of her full name—a reminder of intimate moments that were long gone. She raked his steady gaze with blistering scepticism. The amber eyes burned straight back at her, denying the slightest shift in what he had just declared.

'Another *charming episode* over?' she sliced at him.

He frowned, probably having forgotten how he had described his relationship with her. Whether he recollected it or not, he shot her a look that was loaded with determined purpose. 'Not so charming. In fact, it convinced me I should free myself up to look for something else.'

His gaze moved to Theo, softening as he said, 'Perhaps I should become a father.'

Tina's spine crawled with apprehension. This was the last thing she wanted. The very last! Somehow she had to fight him, convince him that fatherhood would not suit him at all.

'I don't have a father,' Theo gravely informed him. 'I had a grandfather but he got sick and went to heaven.'

'I'm sorry to hear that,' Ari said sympathetically.

'I think people should be aware there's a very real and lasting responsibility about becoming a parent,'

Tina quickly stated, hoping to ward off any impulsive act that would end up badly.

'I agree with you,' Ari said blandly.

'Fly-by-night people shouldn't even consider it,' she persisted, desperately determined on pricking his conscience.

'What are fly-by-night people, Mama?' Theo asked curiously.

Ari leaned forward to answer him. 'They're people who come and go without staying around long enough to really be an important part of your life. They don't stick by you like your mother does. And your grandmother. And your friends. Do you have some friends, Theo?'

'I have lots of friends,' Theo boasted.

'Then I think you must be a happy boy.'

'Very happy,' Tina cut in, giving Ari a look that clearly telegraphed *without you*.

'Then you must be a very special mother, Christina,' he said in his soft, seductive voice. 'It could not have been easy for you, bringing him up alone.'

She bridled at the compliment. 'I wasn't alone. My parents supported me.'

'Family,' he murmured, nodding approvingly. 'So important. One should never turn one's back on family.'

The glittering challenge in his eyes spurred her into leaning over to privately mutter, 'You turned your back first, Ari.'

'I never have to any blood relative I knew about,' he shot back, leaning towards her and keeping his voice low enough for Theo not to hear his words. 'We can do this the easy way or the hard way, Christina.'

'Do what?'

'Fighting over him is not in our son's best interests.'

'Then don't fight. Let him be.'

'You expect me to ignore his existence?'

'Why not? You've ignored mine.'

'A mistake. Which I will correct.'

'Some mistakes can never be corrected.'

'We shall see.'

The fight was on!

No avoiding it.

The rush of blood to her head as she'd tried to argue him out of it drained away, leaving her dizzy and devastated by his resolute counter to everything she'd said.

He straightened up and smiled at Theo who was tucking into a slice of watermelon. 'Good?' he asked.

Theo nodded, his mouth too full to speak but his eyes twinkling a smile back at Ari. Tina seethed over his charming manner to her son. He'd been so very charming to her once. It meant *nothing!* But it was impossible to explain that to a five-year-old boy.

Ari turned his attention back to her. 'Cassandra told me you now manage a restaurant at Bondi Beach.'

'Yes. It was my father's. He trained me to take over when…when he could no longer do it himself.' Another bad time in her life but she had coped. The restaurant was still thriving.

'That surely means working long hours. It must be difficult, being a mother, too.'

She glared at him, fiercely resenting the suggestion

she might be neglecting her son. 'We live in an apartment above the restaurant. Theo attends a pre-school,
which he loves, during the day. He can be with me or
my mother at all other times. And the beach is his play-
ground, which he also loves. As you remarked, he is a
happy boy.'

And he doesn't need you. For anything.

'Mama and I build great sandcastles,' Theo informed
him.

'There are lots of beaches on the Greek islands,' Ari
said.

'Can anyone go on them?' Theo asked.

'There are public beaches which are for everyone.'

'Do they have chairs in rows like we saw in Dubai?'

'The private beaches do.'

'I don't like that.'

'There's one below where I live on Santorini that
doesn't have chairs. You could build great sand-castles
there.'

'Would you help me?'

Ari laughed, delighted he had won Theo over.

'I don't think we'll have time for that,' Tina said
quickly.

'Nonsense!' Ari grinned triumphantly at her.
'Cassandra told me you're spending five days on
Santorini, and Theo's birthday is two days before the
wedding. It would be my pleasure to give Theo a wonderful time—a trip on the cable-car, a ride on a donkey...'

'A donkey!' Theo cried excitedly.

'...a boat-ride to the volcanic island...'

'A boat-ride!' Theo's eyes were as big as saucers.

'...and a trip to a beach where we can build the biggest sandcastle ever!'

'Can we, Mama? Can we?'

His voice was so high-pitched with excitement, it drew her mother's attention. 'Can you what, Theo?' she asked indulgently.

'Ride a donkey and go on a boat, Yiayia. For my birthday!'

'I said I would take him,' Ari swiftly slid in. 'Give him a birthday on Santorini he will always remember.'

'How kind of you!' Her mother beamed at him—the man gorgeous enough to be a movie star, giving his time to make her grandson's stay on Santorini so pleasurable!

The trap was shut. No way out. With both her mother and Theo onside with Ari, Tina knew she would just have to grit her teeth and go along with him. Being a spoilsport would necessitate explanations she didn't want to give. Not at this point. He might force her to make them in the very near future but she would keep it a private issue between them as long as she could.

Cass didn't deserve to have her wedding overshadowed by a situation that should never have arisen. With that one crazy urge to slap Ari with the truth in Dubai... but the damage was done and somehow Tina had to contain it. At least until after the wedding.

With the whole family's attention drawn to them, she forced herself to smile at Ari. 'Yes, very kind.'

'Cassandra mentioned you'll be staying at the El Greco resort,' he said, arrogantly confident of her agree-

ment to the plan. 'I'll contact you there, make arrangements.'

'Fine! Thank you.'

With that settled, conversation picked up around the
table again and Theo plied Ari with questions about
Santorini, which were answered with obvious good hu-
mour.

Tina didn't have to say anything. She sat in brooding
silence, hating Ari Zavros for his facile charm, hating
herself for being such a stupid blabbermouth, gearing
herself up to tolerate what had to be tolerated and savagely vowing that Ari would not get everything his own
way.

Eventually Cass and George excused themselves
from the party, saying they needed to catch up on some
sleep. To Tina's huge relief, Ari stood up to take his
leave, as well. She rose from her chair as he offered his
hand which she had to be civil enough to take in front
of company.

He actually had the gall to enclose her hand with both
of his with a show of enthusiastic pleasure. 'Thank you
for trusting me with Theo's birthday, Christina.'

'Oh, I'm sure I can trust you to give the best of yourself, Ari,' she answered sweetly, before softly adding
with a touch of acid mockery, 'For a limited time.'

Which told him straight out how very little she
trusted him.

He might have won Theo over—for a day—but he'd
won nothing from her.

'We shall see,' he repeated with that same arrogant
confidence.

General goodnights were exchanged and finally he was gone.

But he'd left his presence behind with her mother raving on about him and Theo equally delighted with the nice man.

No relief from the trap.

Tina had the wretched feeling there never would be.

CHAPTER FOUR

MAXIMUS Zavros sat under the vine-covered pergola at one end of the vast patio which overlooked the Aegean Sea. It was where he habitually had breakfast and where he expected his son to join him whenever Ari was home. Today was no exception. However he was taking no pleasure in his surroundings and none in his son, which was obvious from the dark glower of disapproval he directed at Ari the moment he emerged from the house.

'So, you come home without a woman to marry again!' He folded the newspaper he'd been reading and smacked it down on the table in exasperation. 'Your cousin, George, is two years younger than you. He does not have your engaging looks. He does not have your wealth. Yet he can win himself a wife who will grace the rest of his life.' He threw out a gesture of frustration. 'What is the problem with you?'

'Maybe I missed a boat I should have taken,' Ari tossed at his father as he pulled out a chair and sat down, facing him across the table.

'What is that supposed to mean?'

Ari poured himself a glass of orange juice. This was

going to be a long conversation and his throat was already dry. He took a long sip, then answered, 'It means I've met the woman I must marry but I let her go six years ago and somehow I have to win her again. Which is going to prove difficult because she's very hostile to me.'

'Hostile? Why hostile? You were taught to have more finesse than to leave any woman hostile. And why *must* you marry her? To saddle yourself with a sourpuss will not generate a happy life. I credited you with more good sense than that, Ari.'

'I left her pregnant. Unknowingly, I assure you. She gave birth to a son who is now five years old.'

'A son! A grandson!' The tirade was instantly diverted. His father ruminated over this totally unanticipated piece of news for several minutes before speaking again. 'You're sure he is yours?'

'No doubt. The boy not only has a strong resemblance to me but the birth date places the conception during the time I was with Christina.'

'Who is this Christina? Is it possible she could have been with another man?'

Ari shook his head. 'I can't even entertain that as a possibility. We were too intimately involved at the time. And she was a virgin, Papa. I met her when I was in Australia. She was at the start of a promising modelling career…young, beautiful, utterly captivating. When I concluded my business there I said goodbye to her. I had no plans for marriage at that point in my life and I thought her too young to be considering it, either. I thought her life was just starting to open up for her.'

'Australia…' His father frowned. 'How did you meet again? You haven't been back there.'

'George's wife-to-be, Cassandra…when they stayed overnight in the apartment at Athens, I discovered that she was Christina's sister. Christina is to be bridesmaid at the wedding and her son, Theo—*my* son—is to be page boy. They were already in Athens en route to Santorini and I went to a family party to meet them.'

'Is it known to the family that you are the father?'

'No. They were obviously in ignorance of my involvement. But I cannot ignore it, Papa. Christina wants me to. She is appalled to find herself caught up in a situation with me again.'

'She wants to keep the boy to herself.'

'Yes.'

'So… her mind-set against you has to be changed.'

It was a relief that his father had made a straight leap to this conclusion, although it had been fairly predictable he would arrive at it, given the pull of a grandson.

'I intend to make a start on that tomorrow. It's Theo's fifth birthday and I managed to manipulate an agreement for the two of them to spend it with me.'

'She was not a willing party?'

'I made it unreasonable for her to refuse. The fact that she doesn't want to reveal to her family that I'm Theo's father gives me a lever into her life. At least until after the wedding. I suspect she doesn't want to take any focus off her sister at this time.'

'Caring for her family… I like that. Will she make you a good wife, Ari?'

He made an ironic grimace. 'At least she likes children which cannot be said for Felicity Fullbright. I still find Christina very attractive. What can I say, Papa? I've made my bed and I shall lie in it. When you meet the boy you'll know why.'

'When do they arrive on Santorini?'

'Today.'

'Staying where?'

'The El Greco resort.'

'I shall call the management personally. All expenses for their stay will be paid by me. Fresh fruit and flowers in their rooms. A selection of our best Santorini wines. Everything compliments of the Zavros family. They need to be acquainted with our wealth and power. It tends to bend people's minds in a positive manner.'

Ari kept his own counsel on this point. His father could be right. Generosity might have a benign influence. However, he was well enough acquainted with the Australian character to know they had a habit of cutting down tall poppies. However high people rose on their various totem poles, it did not make them better than anyone else. Apart from which, Christina had already demonstrated a strong independence. He doubted she could be bought.

'The mother might be favourably impressed,' he commented. 'Her name is Helen and she is a widow. It might help if you and Mama pay her some kind attention at the wedding.'

His father nodded. 'Naturally we will do so. As a grandparent she should be sympathetic to those who wish to be. I will make my feelings on the subject known.'

'She is Greek. So was her husband. The two daughters were born and brought up in Australia, but she would be familiar with the old ways…arranged marriages between families. If she understands it could be best for Christina and Theo to have the support and security our family can give them…'

'Leave it to me. I shall win over the mother. You win over the daughter and your son. It is intolerable that we be left out of the boy's life.'

That was the crux of it, Ari thought.

Whatever had to be done he would do to be a proper father to his son.

Ten hours was a long ferry ride from Athens to Santorini. Theo was fascinated by the wake of the boat so Tina spent most of the time on the outer rear deck with him while her mother relaxed inside with a book. They passed many islands, most of them looking quite barren and unattractive, and to Tina's mind, not the least bit alluring like the tropical islands back home. It was disappointing. She had expected more magic. However, these islands were obviously not the main tourist drawcards like Mykonos, Paros, Naxos, and most especially Santorini.

When the ferry finally entered the harbour of their destination, she easily understood the stunning attraction of the landscape created from the volcanic eruption that had devastated ancient civilisations. The water in what had been the crater was a gorgeous blue, the semicircle of high cliffs was dramatic, and perched on top of them the classic white Greek island townships glistened in the late afternoon sunshine.

She wished Ari Zavros did not live on this island. She had looked forward to enjoying it, wanted to enjoy it, and decided she would do so in spite of him. If he had any decency at all, he would let the paternity issue drop, realizing he didn't fit into the life she'd made for herself and Theo, and they were not about to fit into his with his obvious bent for a continual stream of *charming episodes*.

Transport was waiting for them at the ferry terminal. Theo was agog with how the mini-bus would negotiate the amazing zig-zag road which would take them from the bottom of the cliff to the top. As it turned out, the trip was not really hair-raising and the view from the bus-window was beautiful.

The El Greco resort faced the other side of the island, built in terraces down the hillside with rooms built around the swimming pools on each terrace. The buildings were all painted blue and white and the gardens looked very tropical with masses of colourful bougainvillea and hibiscus trees. The reception area was cool and spacious, elegantly furnished and with a view of the sea at the far end. A very attractive place, Tina thought. A place to relax. Except relaxation switched instantly to tension when they started to check in at the reception desk.

'Ah, Mrs Savalas, just a minute please!' the receptionist said quickly, beaming a rather unctuous smile at them. 'I must inform the manager of your arrival.' He ducked away to call through a doorway, 'The Savalas party has arrived.'

A suited man emerged from a back office, beaming a similar smile at them as he approached the desk.

'Is there a problem with our booking?' her mother asked anxiously.

'Not at all, Mrs Savalas. We have put you in rooms on the first terrace which is most convenient to the restaurant and the pool snack-bar. If there is anything that would make you more comfortable, you have only to ask and it will be done.'

'Well, that's very hospitable,' her mother said with an air of relief.

'I have had instructions from Mr Zavros to make you most welcome, Mrs Savalas. I understand you are here for a family wedding.'

'Yes, but...' She threw a puzzled look at Tina whose fists had instinctively clenched at the name that spelled danger all over this situation. 'It's very kind of Ari Zavros to...'

'No, no, it is Maximus Zavros who has given the orders,' the manager corrected her. 'It is his nephew marrying your daughter. Family is family and you are not to pay for anything during your stay at El Greco. All is to be charged to him, so put away your credit card, Mrs Savalas. You will not need it here.'

Her mother shook her head in stunned disbelief. 'I haven't even met this Maximus Zavros.'

It did not concern the manager one bit. 'No doubt you will at the wedding, Mrs Savalas.'

'I'm not sure I should accept this…this arrangement.'

'Oh, but you must!' The manager looked horrified at the thought of refusal. 'Mr Zavros is a very wealthy, powerful man. He owns much of the real estate on Santorini. He would be offended if you did not accept his hospitality and I would be at fault if I did not persuade you to do so. Please, Mrs Savalas… I beg you to enjoy. It is what he wishes.'

'Well…' Her mother looked confused and undecided until a helpful thought struck. She shot Tina a determined look. 'We can talk to Ari about this tomorrow.'

Tina nodded, struggling with the death of any hope that Ari might disappear from her life again. She couldn't believe this was simply a case of a rich powerful Greek extending hospitality. The words—*family is family*—had been like a punch in the stomach. She couldn't dismiss the sickening suspicion that Ari had blabbed to his father. It was the only thing that made sense of this extraordinary move.

'Let me show you to your rooms. A porter will bring your luggage.' The manager bustled out from behind the reception desk. 'I want to assure myself that all is as it should be for you.'

Their adjoining rooms were charming, each one with a walled outside area containing a table and chairs for enjoying the ambience of the resort. Complimentary platters of fresh fruit and a selection of wines were provided. The gorgeous floral arrangements were obvious extras, too. Her mother was delighted with everything. Tina viewed it all with jaundiced eyes and Theo was only interested in how soon he could get into the children's swimming pool.

Their luggage arrived. Tina left her mother in the room Cassandra would share with her the night before the wedding and took Theo into theirs. Within a few minutes she had found their swimsuits in her big suitcase, and feeling driven to get out of the Zavros-permeated room, she and Theo quickly changed their clothes and headed for the water.

She sat on the edge of the shallow pool while Theo dashed in and splashed around, full of happy laughter. Her mind was dark with a terrible sense of foreboding and it was difficult to force an occasional smile at her son. Ari's son. Maximus Zavros's grandson.

Did they intend to make an official claim on him?

People like them probably didn't care how much they disrupted others' lives. If something was desired, for whatever reason, they went after it. And got it. Like the rooms in this resort. Almost anything could be manipulated with wealth.

She couldn't help feeling afraid of the future. She was on this island—their island—for the next five days and it would be impossible to avoid meeting Ari's family at the wedding. Ironically, throwing his fatherhood in his face in Dubai was no longer such a hideous mistake. He would have figured it out at the wedding. There would have been no escape from his knowing. She'd been on a collision course with Ari Zavros from the moment Cassandra had agreed to marry his cousin.

The big question was…how to deal with him?

Should she tell her mother the truth now?

Her head ached from all the possible outcomes of revealing her secret before she absolutely had to. Better to wait, she decided, at least until after she'd spent tomorrow with Ari. Then she would have a better idea of what he intended where Theo was concerned and what she could or couldn't do about it.

Tomorrow… Theo's fifth birthday.

His first with his father.

Tina knew she was going to hate every minute of it.

CHAPTER FIVE

TINA and Theo were about to accompany her mother to breakfast in the nearby restaurant when a call from Ari came through to her room. She quickly pressed her mother to go ahead with Theo while she talked to *the nice man* about plans for the day. As soon as they were out of earshot she flew into attack mode, determined on knowing what she had to handle.

'You've told your father about Theo, haven't you?' she cried accusingly.

'Yes, I have,' he answered calmly. 'He had the right to know, just as I had the right to know. Which you denied me for the past five years, Christina.'

'You made it clear that you were finished with me, Ari.'

'You could have found me. My family is not unknown. A simple search on the Internet...'

'Oh, sure! I can just imagine how much you would have welcomed a cast-off woman running after you. Any contact from me via computer and you would have pressed the delete button.'

'Not if you'd told me you were pregnant.'

'Would you have believed me?' she challenged.

His hesitation gave her instant justification for keeping him in ignorance.

'I thought I had taken care of contraception, Christina,' he said, trying to justify himself. 'I would certainly have checked. However, we now have a different situation—a connection that demands continuation. It's best that you start getting used to that concept because I won't be cut out of my son's life any longer.'

The edge of hard ruthlessness in his tone told her without a doubt that he was intent on making a legal claim. A down to the wire fight over Theo was inevitable. What she needed to do now was buy time. Quelling the threatening rise of panic, she tried bargaining with him.

'You said in Athens we could do this the easy way or the hard way, Ari.'

'Yes. I meant it. Is there something you'd like to suggest?'

'You messed up my life once and I guess nothing is going to stop you from messing it up again. But please…don't make a mess of my sister's day in the sun as a bride. That would be absolutely rotten and selfish, which is typical of your behaviour, but… I'll make it easy for Ari to get to know your son over the next few days if you hold back on telling everyone else you're his father until after the wedding.'

The silence that followed her offer was nerve-wracking. Tina gritted her teeth and laid out *the hard way*. 'I'll fight you on every front if you don't agree, Ari.'

'When was I ever rotten or selfish to you in our relationship?' he demanded curtly, sounding as though his self-image was badly dented.

'You made me believe what wasn't true... for your own ends,' she stated bitingly. 'And may God damn you to hell if you do that to Theo.'

'Enough! I agree to your deal. I shall meet you at the resort in one hour. We will spend the day happily together for our son's pleasure.'

He cut the connection before Tina could say another word. Her hand was shaking as she returned the telephone receiver to its cradle. At least Cass's wedding wouldn't be spoiled, she told herself. As for the rest... the only thing she could do was deal with one day at a time.

It took Ari the full hour to get his head around Christina's offensive reading of his character. Anger and resentment kept boiling through him. He wasn't used to being so riled by any situation with a woman. It was because of Theo, he reasoned. It was only natural that his emotions were engaged where his son was concerned.

As for Christina, her hostility towards him was totally unreasonable. He remembered romancing her beautifully, showering her with gifts, saying all the sweet words that women liked to hear, wining and dining her, not stinting on anything that could give her pleasure. No one could have been a better first lover for her.

Was it his fault that the contraception he'd used had somehow failed to protect her from falling pregnant?

He had never, *never* intended to mess up her life. He would have dealt honourably with the situation had he known about it. She could have been living in luxury all these years, enjoying being part of a family unit instead of struggling along with single parenthood.

That was her decision, not his. She hadn't allowed him a decision. If there was any condemnation of character to be handed out on all of this, it should be placed at her door. It was *selfish* and *rotten* of her to have denied him the joys of fatherhood.

Yet…there was nothing selfish about not wanting anything to spoil her sister's wedding.

And he could not recall her ever making some selfish demand on him during the time they'd spent together. Not like Felicity Fullbright. Very, very different to Felicity Fullbright. A delight to be with in every sense.

Gradually he calmed down enough to give consideration to her most condemning words… *You made me believe what wasn't true…for your own ends.*

What had he made her believe?

The answer was glaringly simple when he thought about it. She'd been very young, inexperienced, and quite possibly she'd interpreted his whole seduction routine as genuine love for her. Which meant she'd been deeply hurt when he'd left her. So hurt, she probably couldn't bear to tell him about her pregnancy, couldn't bear to be faced with his presence again.

And she thought he might hurt Theo in the same way—apparently loving him, then leaving him.

He had to change her perception of him, make her

understand he would never abandon his child. He had to show her that Theo would be welcomed into his family and genuinely loved. As for winning her over to being his wife…trying to charm her into marrying him wasn't likely to work. Those blazing dark eyes of hers would shoot down every move he made in that direction. So what would work?

She had just offered him a deal.

Why not offer her one?

Make it a deal too attractive to refuse.

Ari worked on that idea as he drove to the El Greco resort.

'He looks just like a Greek God,' her mother remarked admiringly as Ari Zavros strode across the terrace to where they were still sitting in the open-air section of the restaurant, enjoying a last cup of coffee after breakfast.

Tina's stomach instantly cramped. She had thought that once—the golden Greek with his sun-streaked hair and sparkling amber eyes and skin that shone like bronze. And, of course, it was still true. The white shorts and sports shirt he wore this morning made him look even more striking, showing off his athletic physique, the masculine strength in his arms and legs, the broad manly chest. The man was totally charismatic.

This time, however, Tina wasn't about to melt at his feet. 'Bearing gifts, as well,' she said ironically, eyeing the package he was carrying under his arm.

'For me?' Theo cried excitedly.

Ari heard him, beaming a wide grin at his son as he

arrived at their table and presented him with the large package. 'Yes, for you. Happy birthday, Theo.'

'Can I open it?' Theo asked, eagerly eyeing the wrapping paper.

'You should thank Ari first,' Tina prompted.

'Thank you very much,' he obeyed enthusiastically.

Ari laughed. 'Go right ahead. Something for you to build when you have nothing else to do.'

It was a Lego train station, much to Theo's delight.

'He loves Lego,' her mother remarked, finding even more favour with the Greek God.

'I thought he would,' Ari answered. 'My nephews do. Their rooms are full of it.'

'Talking of family,' her mother quickly slid in. 'Your father has apparently insisted on paying for all our accommodation here and…'

'It is his pleasure to do so, Mrs Savalas,' Ari broke in with a smile to wipe out her concern. 'If you were staying on Patmos, George's family would see to it. Here, on Santorini, my father is your host and he has asked me to extend an invitation to all of you for dinner tonight at our family home. Then we will not be strangers at the wedding.'

Her mother instantly melted. 'Oh! How kind!'

Tina glared at Ari. Had he lied about keeping the deal? And what of his parents? Had he warned them not to reveal their relationship to Theo? He was pursuing his own agenda and she wasn't at all sure he would respect hers. Far from melting at his *kindness,* every nerve in her body stiffened with battle tension.

Ari kept smiling. 'I've told my mother it's your birthday, Theo. She's planning a special cake with five candles for you to blow out and make a wish. You've got all day to think about what to wish for.'

All day to worm his way into Theo's heart with his facile charm, Tina thought grimly. She knew only too well he could be *Mr Wonderful* for a while. It was the long haul that worried her—how *constant* Ari would be as a father.

'Are you coming with us today, Mrs Savalas?' he asked, apparently happy to have her mother's company, as well, probably wanting the opportunity to get her even more onside with him.

'No, no. It sounds too busy for me. I shall stroll into the township in my own time, take a look at the church where the wedding is to be held, do a little shopping, visit the museum.' She smiled at Tina, her eyes full of encouraging speculation. 'Much better for you young people to go off together.'

Tina barely stopped herself from rolling her own eyes at what was obviously some romantic delusion. Gorgeous man—unmarried daughter—Greek island in the sun.

'I shall look forward to the family dinner tonight,' her mother added, giving whole-hearted approval to Ari's plans for the whole day.

Tina smothered a groan.

No escape.

She had agreed to letting him into their lives in return for his silence until after the wedding, but if he or his parents let the cat out of the bag tonight, she would bite their heads off for putting their self-interest ahead of everything else.

After a brief return to their room to put the Lego gift on Theo's bed, refresh themselves, and collect hats and swimming costumes, they re-met Ari and set off for the five-minute walk into the main township of Fira. Tina deliberately placed Theo between them. He held her hand, and unknowingly, his father's. She wondered how she was going to explain this truth to him—another nail in her heart.

'Are your parents aware of our deal?' she asked Ari over Theo's head.

'They will be in good time,' he assured her.

She had to believe him…until his assurance proved false, like the words he had spoken to her in the past. Would he play fair with her this time? She could only hope so. This wasn't about him. Or her. It was about the life of their child.

The view from the path into town was spectacular, overlooking the fantastic sea-filled crater with its towering cliffs. Two splendid white cruise ships stood in the middle of the glittering blue harbour and Theo pointed to them excitedly.

'Are we going to ride in one of those boats?'

'No, they're far too big to move close to land,' Ari answered. 'See the smaller boats going out to them? They're to take the people off and bring them to the island. We'll be riding in a motor-launch that can take us wherever we want to go. You can even steer it for a while if you like.'

Theo was agog. 'Can I? Can I really?'

Ari laughed. 'You can sit on my lap and be the captain. I'll show you what to do.'

'Did you hear that, Mama? I'll be captain of the boat.'

'Your boat, Ari?' Tina asked, anxiously wondering what other goodies he had up his sleeve, ready to roll out for Theo's pleasure.

'A family boat. It will be waiting for us at the town wharf.'

His family. His very wealthy family. How could she stop the seduction of her son by these people? He was a total innocent, as she had been before meeting Ari. He was bound to be deeply impressed by them and the outcome might be a terrible tug-of-war for his love.

Tina suffered major heartburn as they strolled on into town. It was so easy for Ari to win Theo over. It had been easy for him to win her over. He had everything going for him. Even now, knowing how treacherous it was, she still had to fight the pull of his attraction. After him, no other man had interested her, not once in the years since he had left her behind. While he, no doubt, had had his pick of any number of beautiful women who had sparked his interest. Like the blonde in Dubai and probably dozens of others.

It was all terribly wrong. He had been the only man in her life and she'd meant nothing to him. She only meant something to him now because she was the mother of his child and he had to deal with her.

On the road up to the beautiful white church dominating the hillside, a statue of a donkey stood outside a tourist shop displaying many stands of postcards. The donkey was painted pink and it had a slot for letters in its mid-section. Over the slot was painted a red heart with the words POST OF LOVE printed on it.

'I didn't get to sit on the camel, Mama. Can I sit on this donkey?' Theo pleaded.

'You'll be sitting on a real donkey soon. Won't that be better?' Tina cajoled, mentally shying from anything connected with *love*.

Theo shook his head. 'It won't be pink. I'd like a photo of me on this one.'

'Then we must do it for the birthday boy,' Ari said, hoisting Theo up on the donkey and standing beside him to ensure he sat on it safely.

They both grinned at her, so much a picture of father and son it tore at Tina's heart as she viewed it through the camera and took the requested shot.

'Now if you'll stand by Theo, I'll take one of the two of you together,' Ari quickly suggested.

'Yes! Come on, Mama!' Theo backed him up.

She handed Ari her camera and swapped places with him.

'Smile!' he commanded.

She put a smile on her face. As soon as he'd used her camera he whipped a mobile phone out of his shirt pocket and clicked off another shot of them. To show his parents, Tina instantly thought. *This is the woman who is Theo's mother and this is your grandson.* It would probably answer some fleeting curiosity about her, but they would zero straight in on Theo, seeing Ari in him—a Zavros, not a Savalas.

'You have a beautiful smile, Christina,' Ari said

warmly as he returned her camera and lifted Theo off the donkey.

'Stop it!' she muttered, glaring a hostile rejection at him. She couldn't bear him buttering her up when he probably had some killing blow in mind to gain custody of his son.

He returned a puzzled frown. 'Stop what?'

Theo was distracted by a basket of soft toys set out beside the postcard stands, giving her space enough to warn Ari off the totally unwelcome sweet-talking.

'I don't want any more of your compliments.'

His gesture denied any harm in them. 'I was only speaking the truth.'

'They remind me of what a fool I was with you. I won't be fooled again, Ari.'

He grimaced. 'I'm sorry you read more into our previous relationship than was meant, Christina.'

'Oh! What exactly did you mean when you said I was special?' she sliced back at him, her eyes flashing outright scepticism.

He gave her a look that sent a wave of heat through her, right down to her toes. 'You were special. Very special. I just wasn't ready to take on a long-term relationship at the time. But I am now. I want to marry you, Christina.'

Her heart stopped. She stared at him in total shock. No way had she expected this. It was Theo, her stunned mind started to reason. Ari thought it was the best way—the easiest way—to get Theo. Who *she* was, and what *she* wanted was irrelevant.

'Forget it!' she said tersely. 'I'm not about to change my life for your convenience.'

'I could make it convenient for you, too,' he quickly countered.

Her eyes mocked his assertion. 'How do you figure that?'

'A life of ease. No fighting over Theo. We bring him up together. You'll have ample opportunity to do whatever you want within reason.'

'Marriage to you is no guarantee of that. You can dangle as many carrots as you like in front of me, Ari. I'm not biting.'

'What if I give you a guarantee? I'll have a prenuptial agreement drawn up that would assure you and Theo of financial security for the rest of your lives.' His mouth took on an ironic twist. 'Think of it as fair payment for the pain I've given you.'

'I'm perfectly capable of supporting Theo.'

'Not to the extent of giving him every advantage that wealth can provide.'

'Money isn't everything. Besides, I don't want to be your wife. That would simply be asking for more pain.'

He frowned. 'I remember the pleasure we both took in making love. It can be that way again, Christina.'

She flushed at the reminder of how slavishly she had adored him. 'You think a seductive honeymoon makes a marriage, Ari? Taking me as your wife is just a cynical exercise in legality. It gives you full access to our son. Once you have that, I won't matter to you. You'll meet other women who will be happy to provide you with a *special* experience. Can you honestly say you'll pass that up?'

'If I have you willing to share my bed, and the family I hope we'll have together, I shall be a faithful husband like my father,' he said with every appearance of sincerity.

'How can I believe that?' she cried, sure that his sincerity couldn't be genuine.

'Tonight you will meet my parents. Their marriage was arranged but they made it work. It was bonded in family and they are completely devoted to each other. I see no reason why we cannot achieve that same happiness, given enough goodwill between us. Goodwill for the sake of our son, Christina.'

'Except I don't trust you,' she flashed back at him. 'I have no reason to trust you.'

'Then we can have it written into the prenuptial agreement that should you file for divorce because of my proven infidelity, you will get full custody of our children, as well as a financial settlement that will cover every possible need.'

Tina was stunned again. 'You'd go that far?'

'Yes. That is the deal I'm offering you, Christina.' As Theo moved back to claim their attention, Ari shot her one last purposeful look and muttered, 'Think about it!'

CHAPTER SIX

ARI was deeply vexed with himself. Christina *had* pushed him too far. He should have stuck to the financial deal and not let her mocking mistrust goad him into offering full custody if he didn't remain faithful to their marriage. It was impossible to backtrack on it now. If she remained cold and hard towards him, he'd just condemned himself to a bed he certainly wouldn't want to lie in for long.

The will to win was in his blood but usually his mind warned him when the price to be paid was becoming unacceptable. Why hadn't he weighed it up this time? It was as though he was mesmerised by the fierce challenge emanating from her, the dark blaze of energy fighting him with all her might, making him want to win regardless of the cost.

The stakes were high. He wanted his son full-time, living in his home, not on the other side of the world with visits parcelled out by a family law-court. But something very strong in him wanted to win Christina over, too. Maybe it was instinct telling him she could make him the kind of wife he'd be happy to live with—

better than any of the other women he knew. She'd proved herself a good mother—a deeply caring mother. As for the sharing his bed part, surely it wouldn't prove too difficult to establish some workable accord there.

She'd been putty in his hands once, a beautiful rose-bud of a girl whose petals he had gradually unfurled, bringing her to full glorious bloom. She was made of much stronger stuff now. The power of her passion excited him. It was negative passion towards him at the moment, but if he could turn it around, push it into a positive flow…

She did have a beautiful smile. He wanted to make it light up for him. And he wanted to see her magnificent dark eyes sparkling with pleasure—pleasure in him. The marriage bed need not be cold. If he could press the right buttons…he had to or he'd just proposed the worst deal of his life.

He took stock of this different Christina as they wandered through the alleys of shops leading up to the summit of the town. The short hair did suit her, giving more emphasis to her striking cheekbones and her lovely long neck. Her full-lipped mouth was very sexy—bee-stung lips like Angelina Jolie's, though not quite as pronounced. She wasn't quite as tall as her sister, nor as slim. She was, in fact, very sweetly curved, her breasts fuller than when she was younger, her waist not as tiny—probably because of childbirth—but still provocatively feminine in the flow to her neatly rounded hips.

Today she was wearing a pretty lemon and white striped top that was cut into clever angles that spelled designer wear—possibly a gift from Cassandra. She'd teamed it with white Capri pants and she certainly had the legs to wear them with distinction—legs that Ari wanted wound around him in urgent need. She could make him a fine wife, one he would be proud to own, one he wouldn't stray from if she let herself respond to him.

He would make it happen.

One way or another he had to make it happen.

Marriage! Never in her wildest imagination had Tina thought it might be a possibility with Ari Zavros, not since he'd left Australia, putting a decisive end to any such romantic notion. But this wasn't romance. It was a coldly calculated deal to get what he wanted and he probably thought he could fool her on the fidelity front.

How on earth could she believe he wouldn't stray in the future? Even as they strolled along the alleys filled with fascinating shops women stared at him, gobbling him up with their eyes. When she stopped to buy a pretty scarf, the saleswoman kept looking at him, barely glancing at Tina as she paid for it.

The man was a sex magnet. Despite how he'd left her flat, she wasn't immune to the vibrations, either, which made it doubly dangerous to get involved with him on any intimate level. He'd only hurt her again. To marry him would be masochistic madness. But it was probably best to pretend to be thinking about *his* deal until after Cass's wedding to ensure he kept *her* deal.

Then the truth could come out without it being such a distracting bombshell and visitation rights could be discussed. She wouldn't deny him time with his son since he seemed so intent on embracing fatherhood, but he would have to come to Australia for it. Greece was not Theo's home and she wasn't about to let that be changed.

They reached the summit of the town where a cable-car ran down to the old port. Alternatively one could take a donkey-ride along a zig-zag path from top to bottom. Tina would have much preferred to take the cable-car. Ari, however, was bent on making good his promise to Theo, and she made no protest as he selected three donkeys for them to ride—the smallest one for their son, the biggest one for himself and an average-sized one for her.

Theo was beside himself with excitement as Ari lifted him onto the one chosen for him. Tina quickly refused any need for his help, using a stool to mount her donkey. She didn't want to feel Ari's hands on her, nor have him so close that he would have a disturbing physical effect on her. She'd been unsettled enough by his ridiculous offer of marriage.

He grinned at her as he mounted his own donkey, probably arrogantly confident of getting his own way, just as he was getting his own way about Theo's birth-day. She gave him a *beautiful* smile back, letting him think whatever he liked, knowing in her heart she would do what *she* considered best for her child, and being a miserable mother in a miserable marriage was definitely not best.

'I'll ride beside Theo,' he said. 'If you keep your

donkey walking behind his, I'll be able to control both of them.'

'Are they likely to get out of control?' she asked apprehensively.

'They're fed at the bottom and some of them have a tendency to bolt when they near the end of the path.'

'Oh, great!'

He flashed another confident grin. 'Don't worry. I'll take care of you both. That's a promise, Christina.'

His eyes telegraphed it was meant for the future, too.

He could work overtime on his deal, making it as attractive as he could, but she wasn't having any of it, Tina thought grimly. However, she did have to concede he kept their donkeys at a controlled pace when others started to rush past them. And he cheerfully answered Theo's constant questions with all the patience of an indulgent father.

Her son was laughing with delight and giving Ari an impulsive hug as he was lifted off the donkey. For Tina, it was a relief to get her feet back on solid ground. She'd been far too tense to enjoy her ride.

'We'll take the cable-car back up when we return,' Ari said soothingly, aware of her unease.

She nodded, muttering, 'That would be good.'

'Which boat is ours?' Theo asked, eagerly looking forward to the next treat.

Ari pointed. 'This one coming into the wharf now.'

'Looks like you already have a captain,' Tina remarked.

'Oh, Jason will be happy to turn the wheel over to Theo while he's preparing lunch for us. It will be an easy day for him. When the boat is not in family use, he takes out charters, up to eight people at a time. Today he only has three to look after.'

The good-humoured reply left her nothing to say. Besides, she was sure everything on board would run perfectly for Theo's pleasure. Ari would not fail in his mission to have his son thinking the *nice* man was absolutely wonderful. He'd been wonderful to her for three whole months without one slip for any doubt about him to enter her head.

The white motor launch was in pristine condition. A blue and white striped canopy shaded the rear deck which had bench seats softened by blue and white striped cushions. Tina was invited to sit down and relax while Jason got the boat under way again and Ari took Theo to fetch drinks and give him a tour of the galley.

She sat and tried to concentrate on enjoying the marvellous view, let the day flow past without drawing attention to herself. Tonight's family dinner would test her nerves to the limit, but at least her mother would be there, helping to keep normal conversation rolling along. And despite the stress this meeting with Ari's parents would inevitably cause, Tina told herself she did need to see the Zavros home environment, check that it would be a good place for Theo to be if visits to Santorini had to be arranged.

She smiled as she heard Theo say, 'I'm not allowed to have Coca-Cola. Mama says it's not good for me. I can have water or milk or fruit-juice.'

Welcome to the world of parenting, Ari. It isn't all fun and games. Making healthy choices for your child

*is an important part of it. Would he bother to take that
kind of care or would he hire a nanny to do the real
business of parenting?*

Tina mentally ticked that off as an item to be discussed before agreeing to visits.

'Okay, what would you like?' he asked, not questioning her drinks ruling.

'Orange juice.'

'And what does your Mama like?'

'Water. She drinks lots of water.'

'No wine?'

Not since you put intoxicating bubbles in my brain.

'No. It's water or coffee or tea for Mama,' Theo said
decisively.

'Well, after our hot walk, I guess iced water would
be the best choice.'

'Yes,' Theo agreed.

He carried out jugs of orange juice and iced water,
setting them on the fixed table which served the bench
seats. Theo brought a stack of plastic glasses, carefully separating them out as Ari returned to the galley,
emerging again with a platter containing a selection of
cheeses and crackers, nuts, olives and grapes.

'There we are! Help yourselves,' he invited, though
he did pour out the drinks for them—water for him, too.

'I love olives,' Theo declared, quickly biting into one.

'Ah! A true Greek,' Ari said proudly.

Tina instantly bridled. 'Theo is an Australian.'

'But Yia Yia is Greek, Mama,' Theo piped up.

'Definitely some Greek blood there,' Ari declared,

a glittering blast from his golden eyes defying Tina's claim.

'True,' she agreed, deciding the point that needed to be made could be driven home when Theo was not present. Australia was their home country. Theo was an Australian citizen. And the family court in Australia would come down on Tina's side. At least she had that in her favour.

Ari chatted away to their son who positively basked in his father's attention. He explained about the volcano as they sailed towards what was left of it, telling the story of what had happened in the far distant past, how the volcano had erupted and destroyed everything. Theo lapped it up, fascinated by the huge disaster, and eager to walk up to the crater when they disembarked there.

Then it was on to the islet of Palea Kameni for a swim in the hot springs—another new exciting experience for Theo. Tina didn't really want to change into her bikini, being far too physically conscious of Ari looking at her to feel comfortable in it, but she liked the idea of letting Theo go alone with him even less. He was *her son* and she was afraid of giving Ari free rein with him without her supervision.

Unfortunately Ari in a brief black swimming costume reduced her comfort zone to nil. His almost naked perfectly proportioned male body brought memories of their previous intimacy flooding back. She'd loved being with him in bed; loved touching him, feeling him, looking at him, loved the intense pleasure he'd given her in so many ways. It had been the best time of her life. It hurt, even now, that it had only been *a charming episode* for him. It hurt even more that she couldn't control the treacherous desire to have him again.

She could if she married him. She probably could anyhow. He'd lusted after her before without marriage in mind. But having sex with him again wouldn't feel the same. She wouldn't be able to give herself to him whole-heartedly, knowing she wasn't the love of his life. There would be too many shadows in any bed they shared.

It was easier to push the memories aside when they were back on the boat and properly dressed again. Ari in clothes was not quite so mesmerising. He and Theo took over the wheel, playing at being captain together, steering the boat towards the village of Oia on the far point of Santorini while Jason was busy in the galley.

They had a delicious lunch of freshly cooked fish and salad. After all the activity and with his stomach full, Theo curled up on the bench seat, his head on Tina's lap and went to sleep. Jason was instructed to keep the boat cruising around until the boy woke. If there was still time to visit Oia, he could then take them into the small port.

'We don't want him too tired to enjoy his birthday party tonight,' Ari remarked to Tina.

'No. I think we should head home when he wakes. We've done all you promised him, Ari. He should have some quiet time, building the Lego train station before more excitement tonight,' Tina said, needing some quiet time for herself, as well. It was stressful being constantly in the company of the man who was intent on breaking into her life again.

'Okay.' He gave her an admiring look. 'You've done a good job with him, Christina. He's a delightful child.'

She gritted her teeth, determined not to be seduced by his compliments, deliberately moving her gaze to the black cliffs ahead of them. 'I think it's important to instill good principles in a child as early as possible,' she said, a sudden wave of resentment towards him making her add, 'I don't want him to grow up like you.'

His silence tore at her nerves but she refused to look at him.

Eventually he asked, 'What particular fault of mine are you referring to?'

'Thinking women are your toys to be picked up and played with as you please,' she answered, wishing he could be honest about himself and honest to her. 'I want Theo to give consideration to how he touches others' lives. I hope when he connects with people he will always leave them feeling good.'

Another long silence.

Out of the corner of her eye she saw Ari lean forward, resting his forearms on his thighs. 'If you had not fallen pregnant, Christina,' he said softly, 'wouldn't I have left you with good memories of our relationship?'

'You left me shattered, Ari,' she answered bluntly. 'My parents had brought me up to be a good girl believing that sex should only be part of a loving relationship. I truly believed that with you and it wasn't so. Then when I realised I was pregnant, it made everything so much worse. I had to bear their disappointment in me, as well as knowing I'd simply been your sex toy for a while.'

In some ways it was a relief to blurt out the truth to him, though whether it meant anything to him or not was unknowable. Maybe it might make him treat her with more respect. She was not a pawn to be moved around at his will. She was a person who had to be dealt with as a person who had the right to determine her own life and this time she would do it according to her principles.

Ari shook his head. He was in a hard place here. He wasn't used to feeling guilty about his actions or the decisions he'd made. It was not a feeling he liked. Christina had just given a perspective on their previous relationship that he'd never considered and quite clearly it had to be considered if he was to turn this situation around.

She was staring into space—a space that only she occupied, shutting him out. Yet her hand was idly stroking the hair of their sleeping son. He was the connection between them—the only connection Ari could count on right now. He was no longer sure he could reach her sexually, though he would still give it a damned good try. In the meantime he had to start redeeming himself in her eyes or she would never allow herself to be vulnerable to the physical attraction which he knew was not completely dead.

He'd felt her gaze on him at the hot springs, saw it quickly flick away whenever he looked at her. She kept shoring up defences against him by reliving how he'd wronged her in the past. Would she ever let that go or would he be paying for his sins against her far into the future?

'I'm sorry,' he said quietly. 'It was wrong of me to take you. I think it was your innocence that made you so entrancing, so different, so special, and the way you looked at me then… I found it irresistible, Christina. If it means anything to you, there hasn't been a woman since whose company has given me more pleasure.'

As he spoke the words which were designed to be persuasive, there was a slight kick in Ari's mind—a jolting realization that he was actually stating the truth. When he'd moved on, he'd mentally set her aside—too young, not the right time for a serious relationship—but the moment he'd recognised her in Dubai, he'd wanted to experience the sweetness of her all over again, especially when he'd just been suffering the sour taste of Felicity Fullbright.

Christina shook her head. She didn't believe him.

'It's true,' he insisted.

She turned to look at him, dark intense eyes scouring his for insincerity. He held her testing gaze, everything within him tuned to convincing her they could make another start, forge a new understanding between them.

'You didn't come back to me, Ari,' she stated simply. 'You forgot me.'

'No. I put you away from me for reasons that I thought were valid at the time but I didn't forget you, Christina. The moment I recognised you in Dubai, the urge to pick up with you again was instant. And that was before you told me about Theo.'

She frowned, hopefully realising the impulse had been there before she had spoken of their son. 'You were with another woman,' she muttered as though that urge was tarnished, too.

'I was already wishing that I wasn't before I saw you. Please…at least believe this of me. It's true.'

For the first time he saw a hint of uncertainty in her eyes. She lowered her long thick lashes, hiding her thoughts. 'Tell me what your valid reasons were.'

'To my mind, we both still had a lot to achieve on our own without ties holding us back from making choices we would have made by ourselves. You'd barely started your modelling career, Christina, and it was obvious you had the promise of making it big on the international scene. As your sister has done.'

Her mouth twisted into a wry grimace as she looked down at their sleeping son. 'If you didn't forget me, Ari, did you ever wonder why I never broke into the international scene?'

'I did expect you to. I thought you had chosen to stay in Australia. Some people don't like leaving everything that is familiar to them.'

'I wasn't worth coming back to,' she murmured, heaving a sigh that made him feel she had just shed whatever progress he had made with her.

'I was caught up dealing with family business these past six years, Christina,' he swiftly argued. 'It's only now…meeting you again and being faced with my own son that my priorities are undergoing an abrupt change.'

'Give it time, Ari,' she said dryly. 'They might change again.'

'No. I won't be taking my marriage proposal off the table. I want you to consider it very seriously.'

She slid him a measuring look that promised nothing. 'I'll think about it. Don't ask any more of me now.' She nodded down at Theo. 'I'm tired, too. Please ask Jason to head back to Fira.'

'As you wish,' he said, rising from the bench seat to do her bidding.

Trying to push her further would not accomplish any more than he had already accomplished today. She didn't trust him yet but at least she was listening to him. Tonight would give him the chance to show her the family environment he wanted to move her and Theo into. He had to make it as attractive as he could.

CHAPTER SEVEN

WHILE Theo was occupied fitting the pieces of the Lego train station together, Tina tried to imagine what her life might have been like if she hadn't fallen pregnant. Would she have picked herself up from the deeply wounding disillusionment of her love for Ari and channelled all her energy into forging a successful modelling career?

Almost certainly.

She had been very young—only eighteen at the time—and having been rejected by him she would have wanted to *show* him she really was special—so special he would regret not holding onto her.

Cassandra would have helped her to get a foot in on the international scene. Given the chance, she would have tried to make it to the top, delivering whatever was required to keep herself in demand and in the public eye; fashion shows, magazine covers, celebrity turn-outs that would give her even more publicity. Ambition would have been all fired up to make Ari have second thoughts about his decision, make him want to meet her again.

When and if he did she would have played it very cool. No melting on the spot. She would have made him chase her, earn her, and she wouldn't have given in to him until he'd declared himself helplessly in love with her and couldn't live without her. He would have had to propose marriage.

Which he'd done today.

Except the circumstances were very different to what might have been if Theo had never been conceived. That completely changed the plot, making the marriage proposal worth nothing to her.

Though Ari's face had lit up with pleasure at seeing her in Dubai.

But that was only a *fond memory* rekindled.

She wasn't the same naive, stars-in-her-eyes girl and never would be again, so it was impossible for him to recapture the pleasure he'd had in her company in the past. Surely he had to realise that. Empty words, meaning nothing.

She shouldn't let herself be affected by anything he said. Or by his mega sex appeal which was an unsettling distraction, pulling her into wanting to believe he was sincere when he was probably intent on conducting a softening-up process so she would bend to his will. It was important to keep her head straight tonight. He had rights where Theo was concerned. He had none over her.

It was still very hot outside their room when it came time to dress for the birthday party. Her mother, of course, was wearing black—a smart tunic and skirt with an array of gold jewellery to make it look festive.

Tina chose a red and white sundress for herself, teaming it with white sandals and dangly earrings made of little white shells.

She put Theo in navy shorts, navy sandals, and a navy and white top with red stripes across the chest. He insisted on having the big red birthday badge with the smiley face and the number 5 pinned onto it. Ari had bought it for him this morning on their stroll around the shops and Theo wore it proudly.

'See!' he cried, pointing to his badge when Ari came to pick them up.

Ari laughed, lifted him up high, whirled him around, then held him against his shoulder, grinning at him as he said, 'It's a grand thing to be five, Theo.'

There was little doubt in Tina's mind that Theo would love to have Ari as his Papa. Her heart sank at the thought of how much would have to change when the truth had to be admitted. Ari's parents already knew. She could only hope they would handle this meeting with care and discretion.

To her immense relief, Ari seated her mother beside him on the drive to his home on the other end of the island. It was near the Santo winery, he said. Which reminded Tina that he had come to Australia on a tour of the wine industry there. As they passed terraces of grapevines, it was fascinating to see the vines spread across the ground instead of trained to stand in upright rows. To protect the grapes from the strong winds, Ari explained to her mother who happily chatted to him the whole way.

Eventually they arrived at the Zavros home. The

semicircular driveway was dominated by a fountain with three mermaids as its centrepiece, which instantly fascinated Theo. The home itself appeared to be three Mediterranean-style villas linked by colonnades. Naturally it was white, like most of the buildings on Santorini. Ari led them to the central building which was larger than the other two. It all shrieked of great wealth. Intimidating wealth to Tina.

'We're dining on the terrace,' he informed them, shepherding them along a high spacious hallway that clearly bisected this villa.

The floor was magnificently tiled in a pattern of waves and seashells. They emerged onto a huge terrace overlooking the sea. In front of them was a sparkling blue swimming pool. To the left was a long vine-covered pergola and Tina's heart instantly kicked into a faster beat as she saw what had to be Ari's parents, seated at a table underneath it.

They rose from their chairs to extend a welcome to their guests. Tension whipped along Tina's nerves as both of them looked at Theo first. However their attention on him didn't last too long. They greeted her mother very graciously and waited for her to introduce her daughter and grandson.

Maximus Zavros was an older version of Ari in looks. His wife, Sophie, was still quite a striking woman with a lovely head of soft wavy hair, warm brown eyes and a slightly plump, very curvaceous figure. Although they smiled at her as she was introduced, Tina was acutely conscious of their scrutiny—sizing her up as the mother of their grandson. It was a relief when they finally turned their gaze to Theo again.

'And this is the birthday boy,' Sophie Zavros said indulgently.

'Five!' Theo said proudly, pointing to his badge. Then he gave Ari's father a curious look. 'Your name is Maximus?'

'Yes, it is. If it is easier for you, tonight you can call me Max,' he invited, smiling benevolently.

'Oh, no! I *like* Maximus,' Theo said with a broad smile back. 'Mama took me to a movie about a girl with very long hair. What was her name, Mama?'

'Rapunzel,' Tina supplied, barely stopping herself from rolling her eyes at what was bound to come next.

'Rapunzel,' he repeated. 'But the best part of the movie was the horse. His name was Maximus and he was a great horse!'

'I'm glad he was a great horse,' Ari's father said, amused by the connection.

'He was so good at everything!' Theo assured him. 'And he saved them in the end, didn't he, Mama?'

'Yes, he did.'

Ari's father crouched down to Theo's eye level. 'I think I must get hold of this movie. Maybe you and I could watch it together sometime. Would you like to see it again?'

Theo nodded happily.

'Well, I'm not a horse but I can give you a ride over to the table.'

He swept his grandson up in his arms and trotted him to the table, making Theo bubble with laughter. It star-

tled Tina that such a powerful man would be so play-
ful. Her mother and Sophie were laughing, too—any
awkwardness at meeting strangers completely broken.
She glanced at Ari who was also looking on in amuse-
ment.

He quickly moved closer to her, murmuring, 'Relax,
Christina. We just want to make this a special night for
Theo.'

'Have you told them of your plan to marry me?' she
asked quickly, wanting to know if she was being sized
up as a possible daughter-in-law.

'Yes, but there will be no pressure for you to agree
tonight. This is a different beginning for us, Christina,
with our families involved, because it is about family
this time.'

His eyes burned serious conviction into hers.

It rattled her deep-seated prejudice against believing anything he said. She sucked in a deep breath and
tried to let her inner angst go. This *was* a different scenario between them with their families involved. She
decided to judge the night on its merits, see how she
felt about it afterwards. To begin with she told herself
to be glad that Ari's parents were the kind of people
Theo could take to because there was no avoiding the
fact they would feature in his future.

Maximus Zavros had seated Theo in the chair on
the left of his own at the head of the table. Sophie ush-
ered Tina's mother to the chair next to Theo's and to
the right of her own chair at the foot of the table. Ari
guided Tina to the chair opposite Theo's, putting her
next to his father before sitting beside her.

As soon as they were all seated a man-servant appeared, bringing two platters of hors d'oeuvres. Another followed, bringing jugs of iced water and orange juice.

Ari's father turned to her, pleasantly asking, 'Can I persuade you to try one of our local wines?'

She shook her head. 'No, thank you. I prefer water.'

He looked at her mother. 'Helen?'

'I'm happy to try whatever you suggest, Maximus. I've tasted two of the wines that were sent to my room and they were quite splendid.'

'Ah, I'm glad they pleased your palate.' He signalled to the servant to pour the chosen wine into glasses while he himself filled Tina's glass with water and Theo's with orange juice. He beamed a smile at his grandson. 'Ari tells me you can swim like a fish.'

'I love swimming,' was his enthusiastic reply.

'Did your Mama teach you?'

Theo looked at Tina, unsure of the answer. 'Did you, Mama?'

'No. I took you to tadpole classes when you were only nine months old. You've always loved being in water and you learnt to swim very young.' She turned to Maximus. 'It's important for any child to be able to swim in Australia. There are so many backyard pools and every year there are cases of young children drowning. Also, we live near Bondi Beach, so I particularly wanted Theo to be safe in the water.'

'Very sensible,' Maximus approved, nodding to the pool beyond the pergola. 'There will be no danger for him here, either.'

That was just the start of many subtle and not so

subtle points made to her throughout the evening, by both of Ari's parents. They were clearly intent on welcoming their grandson into their life, assuring her he would be well taken care of and greatly loved. And not once was there any hint of criticism of her for keeping them in ignorance of him until now.

She fielded a few testing questions from Maximus about her own life, but for the most part Ari's parents set out to charm and Tina noticed her mother having a lovely time with Sophie, discussing the forthcoming wedding and marriage in general.

After the hors d'oeuvres, they were served souvlaki and salad which Theo had informed Ari on the boat was his favourite meal. Then came the birthday cake and Ari reminded Theo to make a wish as he blew out the candles—all five of them in one big burst. Everyone clapped and cheered at his success.

The cake was cut and slices of it were served around the table. It was a rich, many layered chocolate cake, moist and delicious, and Theo gobbled his piece up, the first to finish.

'Will I get my wish?' he asked Ari.

'I hope so, Theo. Although if you were wishing for a horse like Maximus, that might be asking for too much.'

'Is wishing for a Papa too much?'

Tina's hands clenched in her lap. Her lungs seized up. The silence around the table felt loaded with emotional dynamite.

'No, that's not asking for too much,' Ari answered decisively.

Her mother leaned over and pulled Theo onto her

lap, giving him a cuddle. 'You miss your Papou, don't you, darling?' She gave Sophie a rueful smile. 'My husband died a year ago. He adored Theo. We didn't have sons, you see, and having a grandson was like a beautiful gift.'

'Yes. A very beautiful gift,' Sophie repeated huskily, her gaze lingering on Theo for a moment before shooting a look of heart-tugging appeal at Tina.

'I think with Ari giving him such a wonderful time today...' her mother rattled on.

'Ari is very good with children,' Sophie broke in. 'His nephews love being with him. He will make a wonderful father.'

Ostensibly she was speaking to her mother but Tina knew the words were for her. Maybe they were true. He might very well be a wonderful father, but being a wonderful husband was something else.

'Maximus and I very much want to see him settled down with his own family,' Sophie carried on.

'Mama, don't push,' Ari gently chided.

She heaved a sigh which drew Tina's mother into a string of sympathetic comments about young people taking their time about getting married these days.

Tina sat in frozen silence until Ari's father leaned towards her and asked, 'Who is managing your family restaurant while you are away, Christina?'

She had to swallow hard to moisten her throat before answering, 'The head chef and the head waiter.'

'You trust them to do it well?'

'Yes. My father set it up before he died that both men

get a percentage of the profits. It's in their best interests to keep it running successfully.'

'Ah! A man of foresight, your father,' he said with satisfaction.

Tina *knew* he was thinking the restaurant could keep running successfully without her. 'It needs an overall manager and my father entrusted me with that job,' she said with defiant pride.

'Which is a measure of his respect for your abilities, Christina. But as a Greek father myself, I know it was not what he wanted for you.'

His amber eyes burned that certain knowledge into her heart. There was no denying it. Her father had not been against his daughters having a career of their choice but he had believed a woman was only truly fulfilled with the love of a good husband and the love of their children.

It hurt, being reminded of her failure to live up to his expectations of her, but the big word in her father's beliefs was love, and Ari did not love her. She faced his father with her own burning determination. 'I have the right to choose what I do with my life. My father respected that, as well.'

'I don't think the choice is so unequivocal when you are a mother, Christina,' he shot back at her. 'The rights of your child have to be considered.'

'Papa...' Ari said in a low warning voice.

'She must understand this, Ari,' was the quick riposte.

'I do,' Tina told him flatly. 'And I am considering them.' She lowered her voice so as not to be overheard at the other end of the table as she fiercely added, 'I hope you do, too, because I *am* Theo's mother and I always will be.'

She would not allow them to take over her son. She would concede visits but knew she would hate every minute Theo was away from her. Not all their wealth and caring would make any difference to the hole that would leave in her life until he returned to her. Tears pricked her eyes. Her head was swimming with all the difficulties that lay ahead.

'Please, forgive me my trespasses,' Ari's father said gruffly. 'You're a fine mother, Christina. And that will always be respected by our family. The boy is a credit to you. How can I put it? I want very much to enjoy more of him.'

A warm hand slid over one of her clenched fists and gently squeezed. 'It's all right, Christina,' Ari murmured, 'You're amongst friends, not enemies.'

She stared down at his hand, biting her lips as she tried to fight back the tears. He'd offered his hand in marriage, which was the easiest way out of the custody issue, but how could she take it when she felt so vulnerable to what he could do to her—twisting up her life all over again?

She swallowed hard to ease the choking sensation in her throat and without looking at either man, said, 'I want to go back to the resort now, Ari. It's been a long day.'

'Of course.' Another gentle squeeze of her hand. 'It's been good of you to let us spend this time together.'

'Yes. A wonderful evening,' his father chimed in. 'Thank you, Christina.'

She nodded, not wanting to be drawn into another stressful conversation. She felt painfully pressured as it was. Her gaze lifted to check Theo who was now nodding off on her mother's lap.

Ari rose from his chair. 'Helen, Mama… Christina is tired and it looks like Theo is ready for bed, as well. It's time to call it a night. I'll carry him out to the car, Helen.'

Ari's parents accompanied them out to the car, walking beside her mother who thanked them profusely for their hospitality. All three expressed pleasure in meeting up again at the wedding. Both Maximus and Sophie dropped goodnight kisses on Theo's forehead before Ari passed him over to Tina in the back seat. She thanked them for the birthday party and the car door was finally closed on it, relieving some of the tension in her chest.

Theo slept all the way back to the resort and the conversation between Ari and her mother in the front seats was conducted in low murmurs. Tina sat in silence, hugging her child, feeling intensely possessive of him and already grieving over how much she would have to part from him.

Having arrived at El Greco, Ari once again lifted Theo into his arms and insisted on carrying him to their accommodation. Tina did not protest, knowing that to her mother this was the natural thing for a man to do. The problem came when she unlocked her door and instead of passing Theo to her, Ari carried him straight into her room.

'Which bed?' he asked.

She dashed past him to turn back the covers on Theo's bed and Ari gently laid him down and tucked him in, dropping a kiss on his forehead before straightening up and smiling down at his sleeping son, making Tina's heart contract at the memory of Theo's wish for a Papa. He had one. And very soon he had to know it.

Ari turned to her and she instantly felt a flood of electricity tingling through her entire body. He was too close to her, dangerously close, exuding the sexual magnetism that she should be immune to but wasn't. Being in a bedroom with Ari Zavros, virtually alone with him, was a bad place to be. She quickly backed off, hurrying to the door, waving for him to leave.

He followed but paused beside her, causing inner havoc again. He raised a hand to touch her cheek and she flinched away from the contact. 'Just go, Ari,' she said harshly. 'You've had your day.'

He frowned at her unfriendliness. 'I only wanted to thank you, Christina.'

She forced her voice to a reasonable tone. 'Okay, but you can do that without touching me.'

'Is my touch so repellent to you?'

Panic tore through her at how vulnerable she might be to it. She stared hard at him, desperate not to show him any weakness. 'Don't push it, Ari. I've had enough, today.'

He nodded. 'I'll call you in the morning.'

'No! Tomorrow is *my* family day,' she said firmly. 'Cassandra will be joining us and so will all our relatives from the mainland. We'll meet again at the wedding.'

For one nerve-wracking moment she thought he would challenge her decision. It surprised her when he smiled and said, 'Then I'll look forward to the wedding. Goodnight, Christina.'

'Goodnight,' she repeated automatically, watching him in a daze of confusion as he walked away from her.

He hadn't done anything *wrong* all day. For the most part, he'd been perfectly charming. And she still *wanted* him, despite the grief he'd given her. There had never been any other man who made her feel what he did. But he probably made every woman feel the same way. It meant nothing. It would be foolish to let it cloud her judgement.

When Theo was told that Ari was his Papa, he would want them to be all together, living happily ever after.

But that was a fairy-tale and this story didn't have the right ingredients. The prince did not love the princess, so how could there be a happy ever after?

Tina fiercely told herself she must not lose sight of that, no matter what!

CHAPTER EIGHT

ARI stood beside George in the church, impatient for the marriage service to be over, his mind working through what had to be accomplished with Christina. Theo was not a problem. His son had grinned broadly at him as he had carried the cushion with the wedding rings up the aisle. He would want his Papa. But Christina had only smiled at George, keeping her gaze averted from him.

She looked absolutely stunning in a dark red satin gown. Desire had kicked in so hard and fast Ari had struggled to control the instinctive physical response to instantly wanting her in his bed again. 'She is magnificent, is she not?' George had murmured, meaning his bride, and she was, but Cassandra stirred nothing in him.

There were many beautiful women in the world. Ari had connected to quite a few of them, but none had twisted his heart as it was being twisted right now. He had to have Christina again. Perhaps she touched something deep in him because she was the mother of his child. Or perhaps it was because he had taken her innocence and she made him feel very strongly about righting the wrong he had done her. The reasons didn't matter. Somehow he had to persuade her to be his wife.

His parents certainly approved of the marriage and not only because of Theo.

'She's lovely, Ari, and I could be good friends with Helen,' his mother had remarked.

His father had been more decisive in his opinion. 'Beautiful, intelligent, and with a fighting spirit I admire. She's a good match for you, Ari. Don't let her get away from you. The two of you should have many interesting children together.'

Easier said than done, Ari thought grimly.

She didn't want him to touch her.

Today, she didn't want to look at him.

Was she frightened of the attraction she still felt with him, frightened of giving in to it? She would *have* to look at him at the wedding reception *and* suffer his touch during the bridal waltz. Not just a touch, either. Full body contact. He would make the waltz one of the most intimate dances she'd ever had, force the sexual chemistry between them to the surface so she couldn't hide from it, couldn't ignore it, couldn't deny it.

She was not going to get away from him.

Tina listened to the marriage service as she stood beside her sister. These same words could be spoken to her soon if she said *yes* to Ari's proposal. Would he take the vows seriously, or were they just mumbo-jumbo to him—the means to an end?

He *had* offered the fidelity clause in a prenuptial agreement. She would get full custody of Theo and any

other children they might have together if he faltered
on that front. Could she be happy with him if he kept
faith with his marriage deal?

It was a risk she probably shouldn't be considering.
Cass's wedding was getting to her, stirring up feelings
that could land her in a terrible mess. Plus all the marriage talk amongst her Greek relatives yesterday had
kept Ari's offer pounding through her mind—no relief
at all from the connection with him.

Her mother had raved on about how kind he'd been—
taking Tina and Theo out for the day, the birthday party
at his parents' home—which had reminded the relatives
of how attentive he'd been to Tina at the family party
in Athens. Comments on how eligible he was followed,
with speculative looks that clearly said Helen's daughter
might have a chance with him. Being a single mother
was…*so unfortunate.*

Little did they know that Theo was the drawcard, not
her. They would all be watching her with Ari today—
watching, hoping, encouraging. She would have to look
at him soon, take his arm as they followed Cass and
George out of the church, be seated next to him at the
wedding reception, dance with him. The whole thing
was a nightmare with no escape, and it would be worse
when the truth was told.

Her mother would want her to marry Ari.

Her relatives would think her mad if she didn't.

Only Cass might take her side, asking what *she*
wanted, but Cass wouldn't be there. She and George
would be off on their honeymoon. Besides, what Tina
wanted was impossible—utterly impossible to go back

to the time when she had loved Ari with all her heart and believed he loved her. How could she ever believe that now?

She felt a sharp stab of envy as George promised to love Cass for the rest of his life. There was no doubting the fervour in his voice, no doubting Cass, either, as she promised her love in return. A huge welling of emotion brought tears to Tina's eyes as the two of them were declared husband and wife. She wished them all the happiness in the world. This was how it should be between a man and a woman, starting out on a life together.

She was still blinking away the wetness in her eyes when she had to link up with Ari for the walk out of the church. He wound her arm around his and hugged her close, instantly causing an eruption of agitation inside Tina.

'Why do women always weep at weddings?' he murmured, obviously wanting her to focus on him.

She didn't. She swept her gaze around the gathered guests, swallowed hard to unblock her voice and answered, 'Because change is scary and you hope with all your heart that everything will work out right.'

'What is right in your mind, Christina?' he persisted.

Christina...he invariably used her full name because it was what she had called herself for the modelling career that had been cut short after he had left her pregnant. During the months they'd spent together she'd loved how that name had rolled off his tongue in a caressing tone. She wished he wouldn't keep using the same tone now, that he'd call her Tina like everyone else. Then she wouldn't be constantly reminded of the girl she had been and how much she had once loved him.

She wasn't that girl any more.

She'd moved on.

Except Ari could still twist her heart and shoot treacherous excitement through her veins.

It was wrong for him to have that power. *Wrong!* And the pain of her disillusionment with him lent a vehement conviction to her voice as she answered him. 'It's right if they keep loving each other for the rest of their lives, no matter what happens along the way.' She looked at him then, meeting the quizzical amber eyes with as much hard directness as she could muster. 'We don't have that basis for marriage, do we?'

'I don't believe that love is the glue that keeps a marriage together,' he shot back at her. 'It's a madness that's blind to any sensible judgement and it quickly burns out when people's expectations of it aren't met. Absolute commitment is what I'm offering you, Christina. You can trust that more than love.'

His cynical view of love was deeply offensive to her, yet she felt the strength of his will encompassing her, battering at her resistance to what he wanted. 'I'd rather have what Cass and George have than what you're offering,' she muttered, resenting the implication that her sister's happiness with her marriage wouldn't last.

'I understand that change must be scary to you, Christina,' he murmured in her ear. 'I promise you I'll do all I can to make the transition easy for both you and Theo.'

The transition! He expected her to give up her life in Australia—all she'd known, all she'd worked for—to be with him. It wouldn't work the other way around. She knew that wouldn't even be considered. She was supposed to see marriage to him as more desirable than anything else, and she would have seen it that way once, *if he'd loved her.*

That was the sticking point.

Tina couldn't push herself past it.

The hurt that he didn't wouldn't go away.

Outside the church they had to pose for photographs. Tina pasted a smile on her face. Her facial muscles ached from keeping it there. Ari lifted Theo up to perch against his shoulder for some shots and everywhere she looked people seemed to be smiling and nodding benevolently at the grouping of the three of them—not as bridesmaid, best man and page boy, but as wife, husband and son. Ari's parents stood next to her mother and Uncle Dimitri. They would all be allied against her if she decided to reject the marriage proposal.

She ached all over from the tension inside her. At least the drive to the reception spared her any active pressure from Ari. Theo rode in their car, sitting between them on the back seat, chatting happily to the man he would soon know as his father. Tina was grateful not have to say anything but she was acutely aware of Theo's pleasure in Ari and Ari's pleasure in his son. How could she explain to a five-year-old boy why they couldn't all be together with the Papa he had wished for?

They arrived at the Santo winery. Its reception centre was perched on top of a cliff overlooking the sea. To the side of the dining section was a large open area shaded by pergolas and normally used for wine-tasting. Guests gathered here while the bridal party posed for more photographs. Waiters offered drinks and canapés. A festive mood was very quickly in full swing.

Tina thought she might escape from Ari's side for a while after the photographer was satisfied but that proved impossible. He led her straight over to George's family who were all in high spirits, delighted to meet their new daughter-in-law's sister and press invitations to be their guest on Patmos at any time.

Then he insisted on introducing her to his sisters and their husbands—beautiful women, handsome men, bright beautiful people who welcomed Tina into their group, making friendly chat about the wedding. Their children, Ari's nephews, all four of them around Theo's age, quickly drew him off with them to play boy games. Which left Tina very much the centre of attention and as pleasant as the conversation was, she knew they were measuring her up as wife material for Ari.

After a reasonable interval she excused herself, saying she should check if Cass needed her for anything.

It didn't provide much of an escape.

'I'll come with you,' Ari instantly said. 'George might require something from me.'

As soon as they were out of earshot, Tina muttered, 'You told them, didn't you?'

'Not the children. Theo won't hear it from them. Keeping it from your family until after the wedding will be respected, Christina. I simply wanted my sisters to understand where you are with me.'

'I'm not anywhere with you,' she snapped defensively, giving him a reproachful glare.

He held her gaze with a blaze of resolute purpose. 'You're my intended wife and I told them so.'

'Why are you rushing into this?' she cried in exasperation. 'We can make reasonable arrangements about sharing Theo. Other people do it all the time. You don't have to *marry* me!'

'I *want* to marry you.'

'Only because of Theo and that's not right, Ari.'

'You're wrong. I want you, too, Christina.'

She shook her head in anguished denial, instantly shying away from letting herself believe him. Cass and George were chatting to a group of their modelling-world friends and Tina gestured to the gorgeous women amongst them. 'Look at what you could have. I'm not in their class. And I bet they'd lap up your attention.'

'You're in a class of your own and I don't want their attention. I want yours.'

'Today you do, but what about the rest of your future, Ari?'

'I'll make my future with you if you'll give it a chance.'

Again she shook her head. There was no point in arguing with him. He had his mind set on a course of action and nothing she said was going to shift him from it.

'It's worth a chance, isn't it, Christina?' he pressed. 'We were both happy when we were intimately in-

volved. It can be that way again. You can't really want
to be separated from Theo during the time he spends
with me if you insist he has to bounce between us.'

She would hate it.

But she was also hating the way Cass's girlfriends
were gobbling Ari up with their eyes, watching him approach the bride and groom. Not that she could blame
them for doing it. He was even more of a sex magnet
today, dressed in a formal dinner suit which enhanced
his perfect male physique, highlighting how stunningly
handsome he was. *A Greek God.* Tina had no doubt they
were thinking that. And envying her for having him at
her side.

Could she stand a lifetime of that with Ari?

Would he always *stay* at her side?

She felt sick from all the churning inside her. Any
distraction from it was intensely welcome. Hopefully
Cass would provide it for a while. She and Ari joined
the celebrity group and were quickly introduced around.
One of George's friends, another photographer, took the
opportunity to give Tina his business card.

'Come to me and I'll turn you into a model as famous
as your sister. No disrespect to you, Cass, but this girl
has quite a unique look that I'd love to capture.'

Cass laughed and turned a beaming smile to Tina.
'I've always said you don't have to be a homebody.'

'But I like being a homebody.' She tried to hand the
card back, embarrassed by the spotlight being turned
on her. 'Thank you, but no.'

'Keep it,' he insisted. 'I mean it. I would love to work

with that wonderful long neck and those marvellous cheekbones. Your short hair sets them off to perfection.'

'No, please, I don't want it. I have nowhere to put your card anyway.'

'I'll keep it for you. You might have second thoughts,' Ari said, taking the card and sliding it into his breast pocket. He smiled around at the group. 'No disrespect to any of you lovely ladies, but I also think Christina is unique. And very special.'

Which was virtually a public declaration of his interest in her, putting off the interest that any of the lovely ladies might want to show in him.

Tina's *marvellous cheekbones* were instantly illuminated by heat.

Cass leaned over to whisper in her ear. 'Mama is right. Ari is very taken by you. Give him a chance, Tina. He's rather special, too.'

A chance!

Even Cass was on Ari's side.

Tina felt the whole world was conspiring to make her take the step she was frightened of taking.

'I think I need some cool air,' she muttered.

Ari heard her. He took her arm. 'Please excuse us, everyone. We're off to catch the sea breeze for a breather.'

He drew her over to the stone wall along the cliff edge. Tina didn't protest the move. It was useless. She was trapped into being Ari's companion at this wedding and he was not about to release her.

'Why did you take that card?' she demanded crossly.

'Because it was my fault that you didn't continue the modelling career you might have had. It's not too late to try again, Christina. You actually have a more individual beauty now. If you'd like to pursue that path you'd have my full support.'

She frowned at him. 'I'm a mother, Ari. That comes first. And isn't it what you want from me, to be the mother of your children?'

'Yes, but there are models who are also mothers. It can be done, Christina.' He lifted his hand and gently stroked her hot cheek, his eyes burning with what seemed like absolute sincerity. 'I destroyed two of your dreams. At least I can give one of them back to you. Maybe the other…with enough time together. '

She choked up.

It was all too much.

Her mind was in a total jumble. She wanted to believe him, yet he couldn't give her back what he had taken. Whatever they had in the future would be different. And was he just saying these things to win her over? She'd trusted him with her heart and soul once and here she was being vulnerable to his seduction again. How could she believe him? Or trust him? She desperately needed to clear her head.

She stepped back from the tingling touch on her cheek and forced herself to speak. 'I'd like a glass of water, Ari.'

He held her gaze for several moments, his eyes searching for what he wanted to see in hers—a softening towards him, cracks in her resistance. Tina silently pleaded for him to go, give her some space, some relief from the constant pressure to give in and take what he was offering.

Finally he nodded. 'I'll fetch you one.'

She stared out to sea, gulping in fresh air, needing a blast of oxygen to cool her mind of its feverish thoughts.

It didn't really work.

Despite her past experience with Ari Zavros, or maybe because of it, one mind-bending thought kept pounding away at her, undermining her resistance to the course he was pressing her to take.

Give it a chance.
Give it a chance.
Give it a chance.

CHAPTER NINE

The bridal waltz...

Tina took a deep breath and rose to her feet as Ari held back her chair. He'd been the perfect gentleman all evening. The speech he'd made preceding his toast to the bride and groom had contained all the right touches, charming the guests into smiling and feeling really good about this marriage. An excellent Best Man.

Maybe he was the best man for her, given that she'd not felt attracted to anyone else in the past six years. If she never connected with some other man... did she want to live the rest of her life totally barren of the sexual pleasure she had known with Ari?

Give it a chance...

As he steered her towards the dance floor, the warmth of his hand on the pit of her back spread a flow of heat to her lower body. The band played 'Moon River,' a slow jazz waltz that Cass and George obviously revelled in, executing it with great panache; gliding, twirling, dipping, making it look both romantic and very, very sexy.

Little quivers started running down Tina's legs as

she and Ari waited for their cue to join in. It had been so long since he had held her close. Would she feel the same wild surge of excitement when she connected to his strong masculinity? It was impossible to quell the electric buzz of anticipation when their cue came and he swept her onto the dance floor, yet she stiffened when he drew her against him, instinctively fighting his power to affect her so *physically*.

'Relax, Christina,' he murmured. 'Let your body respond to the rhythm of the music. I know it can.'

Of course, he knew. There was very little he didn't know about her body and how it responded. And she had to find out what it might be like with him now, didn't she? *If she was to give it a chance.*

She forced herself to relax and go with the flow of the dance. He held her very close; her breasts pressed to his chest, her stomach in fluttering contact with his groin area, her thighs brushing his with every move he made. Her heart was pounding much faster than the beat of the music. Her female hormones were stirred into a lustful frenzy. She was in the arms of a Greek God who was hers for the taking and the temptation to take whatever she could of him was roaring through her.

Ari made the most of Christina's surrender to the dance, hoping the sexual chemistry sizzling through him was being transmitted through every sensual contact point. She felt good in his arms. She was the right height for him, tall enough for their bodies to fit in a very satisfying way as he moved her around the dance floor. The sway of her hips, the fullness of her breasts impacting with their lush femininity, the scent of her skin and hair…everything about her was firing up his desire to have her surrender to him.

The waltz ended. She didn't exactly push out of his embrace but eased herself back enough to put a little distance between them. Her cheeks were flushed and she kept her eyes lowered, their thick black lashes hiding any vulnerable feelings. He was sure she had been physically affected by the intimacy of the dance but whether that was enough to sway her his way he didn't know.

The Master of Ceremonies invited all the guests to dance to the next song which had been especially requested by the bride. Ari instantly understood its significance when the band started playing the tune. He and Christina had heard Stevie Wonder's version of it on the car radio on one of their trips together.

'You are the sunshine of my life,' he said, recalling how he had applied the words to her. 'It's your father's favourite song.'

'Yes,' she said huskily. 'Cass misses him, too. He would have been very proud of her today.' Her lashes lifted and she gave him a wry little smile. 'I'm surprised you remembered.'

'Special songs can be very evocative. You *were* the sunshine of my life while we were together, Christina.'

The smile twisted into a grimace. 'There's been a long night since then, Ari. Though I'm sure you found plenty of sunshine elsewhere.'

'Not of the same quality.'

Her gaze slid away from his. 'We have to dance,' she muttered.

She allowed him to hold her close again without any initial resistance. It was *some* progress, he thought, though he savagely wished she wouldn't keep harping on the other women who'd been in his life. The past was the past—impossible to change it. If she'd just set her sights on the future, that was the progress he needed.

He bent his head closer to hers and murmured, 'What you and I can have *now* is what matters, Christina.'

She didn't answer.

Hopefully she was thinking about it.

Tina fiercely wished she could forget everything else but *now,* pretend she was meeting Ari for the first time, feeling all that he made her feel, her whole body brilliantly alive to exciting sensations. She wouldn't care about the other women if this was her first experience with him. She'd be blissfully thinking that he was the man who could make her life complete.

Maybe he would if she set the pain he'd given her aside. He'd said he wanted to give her back the dreams he'd destroyed. Yet it was a terribly risky step, trusting his word. If he didn't keep it, she would hate herself for being a fool, hate him for his deceit, and end up a totally embittered woman.

But she could make him pay for it.

He would lose Theo and any other children they might have if he broke his promise of fidelity. She wouldn't have to worry over the custody issue. All rights would be hers. In which case, it was worth taking the chance, wasn't it?

Her father's favourite song came to an end. She saw Cass go over to her mother who had danced with Uncle Dimitri and give her a hug and a kiss. It caused a painful drag on Tina's heart. She knew her father would have wanted her to marry Ari. It might have made him proud of her if she did.

She looked up at the man who was her son's father, and the seductive amber eyes instantly locked onto hers, simmering with the promise of all the pleasure they'd once had together. Her heart quivered over the decision she had made but it *was* made and she wasn't going to fret over it any longer.

'Let's go where we can talk privately,' she said firmly.

He nodded, quickly obliging her by steering her off the dance floor, then taking her arm and walking her out to the large open patio where they'd been before the reception dinner.

'Would you like to sit down?' he asked, waving to the wooden tables under the pergola.

'Yes.' Her legs were feeling wobbly. Besides, sitting across from him at a table would be more comfortable for laying out the deal she would accept.

They sat. Ari spread his hands in an open gesture, inviting her confidence. 'What do you want to say, Christina?'

Her hands were tightly clenched in her lap. This was it—the moment when her life would begin to take a totally different direction. A wave of trepidation mangled her vocal chords. She looked hard at him, forcing her imagination to see him as a caring and committed father and husband. If she could believe it, maybe the marriage would work out right. She desperately wanted it to.

The first step was to say the words.

Say them.

Just do it and have done with the whole nerve-wracking dilemma.

'I... I...'

'Yes?' Ari encouraged, leaning forward, giving her his concentrated attention.

A surge of panic had made her hesitate. Her mind was screaming *wait! Don't commit yet!* But what would she be waiting for? The situation wasn't going to change. This man was Theo's father and she had loved him with all her heart once. If he was serious about forging a good relationship with her, shouldn't she give it a chance?

'I'll marry you,' she blurted out, sealing the decision.

His face broke into a happy grin. His eyes sparkled with pleasure. Or was it triumph, having won what he wanted? 'That's great, Christina!' he enthused. 'I'm glad you've decided it's the best course because it is.'

He was *so* positive it instantly raised doubts in Tina's mind. Was she a fool for giving in? She had to put a high value on the marriage so he would treat her as he should.

'Give me your hand,' he pressed, reaching across the table to take it.

She shook her head, keeping both hands tightly in her lap. 'I haven't finished what I want to say.'

He frowned at her reluctance to meet his offered hand. He spread his fingers in open appeal. 'Tell me what you need from me.'

'I need you to sign the prenuptial agreement you offered me,' she threw back at him, determined that those terms be kept. It was her safeguard against being used to give Ari a stronger paternal position than he had now.

He drew back, his mouth twisting into an ironic grimace. A sharp wariness wiped the sparkle from his eyes. Tina's stomach cramped with tension. If he retracted the offer, she could not go ahead with the marriage, regardless of any pressure from any source. It was risking too much. He might walk away from her again and take Theo with him.

She waited for his reply.

Waited…and waited…her nerves stretching tighter with every second that passed.

Ari's mind was swiftly sifting through Christina's possible motivations. She didn't trust his word. He understood where she was coming from on that score. What concerned him most was if she had a vengeful nature.

The prenuptial agreement he'd offered gave her everything if he didn't remain a faithful husband. What if she planned to be such a cold, shrewish wife, he would be driven to find some pleasure in other company? If she was secretly determined not to be responsive to him, he'd be condemning himself to a hellish marriage. He needed more than her public compliance to a couple of dances to feel secure about winning her over in bed.

Out here alone together, she wouldn't even give him her hand.

What was in her mind?

What was in her heart?

A totally selfish revenge on him…or hope that they could make a happy future together?

He was risking a lot.

He decided she had to meet him halfway before he tied a knot which could not be undone.

'I am prepared to sign it, Christina,' he said, his eyes burning a very direct challenge at her as he added, 'If you're prepared to spend one night with me before I do.'

She stared at him, startled by the provision he was laying down. 'Why? You'll have all the nights you want with me after we're married.'

'I want to be sure that I will want them. I won't sign away my right to my son to a woman who'll turn her back on me. I need you to show me that won't happen, Christina. Right now your attitude towards me is hardly encouraging. You won't even give me your hand.'

Heat surged up her neck and scorched her cheeks. Her eyes glittered a challenge right back at him. 'I think it's a good idea for us to spend a night together before either of us commit ourselves to anything. Maybe you're not as good a lover as you used to be, Ari.'

Relief swept through him at her ready acceptance of a sex-test. He smiled. 'And maybe you'll warm to me once I prove that I am.'

Again her lashes swept down, veiling her feelings. She heaved a sigh, probably relieving tension. 'We're scheduled to leave Santorini the day after tomorrow,' she muttered.

'That can easily be changed.'

She shook her head. 'I'll spend tomorrow night with you.' Her lashes lifted and there was resolute fire in her eyes. 'That can be the decider for both of us.'

She would bolt if he didn't satisfy her. Ari was confident that he could if she was willing to let it happen.

'Agreed,' he said. 'However, our other deal ends tonight, Christina. Tomorrow you tell your mother and Theo that I am his father. Whatever happens between us, this has to be openly acknowledged.'

She nodded. 'I'll do it in the morning.'

'Make sure your mother understands the circumstances, that I was not told you had my child until we met in Dubai. I would have come back to you had I known, Christina.'

She made a wry grimace. 'Since I've decided I might marry you, naturally I'll put you in as good a light as possible to my mother.'

'It's the truth,' he rammed home as hard as he could, wanting her to believe at least that much of him.

'And my truth is you left me and I didn't want you back,' she shot out, her eyes glittering with angry pride. 'Don't you start harassing me, Ari. I'll do what I have to do to smooth the path to a workable future.'

His father's words about Christina were instantly replayed in his mind…*beautiful, intelligent, and with a fighting spirit I admire.* If she shared his own strong desire for everything to turn out well, there was no need to concern himself about her presentation of the past to her mother.

'I'd like to be there when you tell Theo I'm his father,' he said softly, needing to remove the anger he'd unwittingly triggered. 'I've missed so much—not being there when he was born, his first words, his first step, learning to swim, his first day at kindergarten. I want to see the expression in his eyes when he realises I am the Papa he wished for. Will you give me that, Christina?'

Her eyes went blank, probably focussing inward on the memories she hadn't shared with him. He willed her to be more generous now. Yet when she did speak, her whole expression was one of deep anxiety.

'I hope you really mean to be a good father to him, Ari. Please don't lead him on and then drop him, pursuing other interests.'

He knew she felt he had done that to her.

It had been wrong of him, letting temptation overrule good sense. She had been too young, too impressionable. Theo was much more so and she was frightened for him. Her fear evoked a powerful surge of emotion in him. He wanted to say he'd look after them both for the rest of his life. He hated seeing the fretful doubts in her eyes. But laying them to rest would take time.

'Give me your hand, Christina,' he gently commanded, his eyes pleading for her acquiescence.

Very slowly she lifted it from her lap and held it out to him.

He enclosed it with his. 'I promise you I'll do everything I can to win Theo's love and keep it,' he said fervently. 'He's my son.'

Tears welled into her eyes. She nodded, unable to speak. He stroked her palm with his thumb, wanting to give comfort and reassurance, wishing he could sweep her into his embrace but cautious about rushing her where she might not be ready to go.

'If it's okay with you, I'll come to the El Greco resort tomorrow afternoon. We can spend some time with Theo before having our night together,' he quietly suggested.

She nodded again, sucked in a deep breath and blurted out, 'I'm sorry. It was mean of me…leaving you out of Theo's life.'

'You had your reasons,' he murmured sympathetically. 'It's how we take it from here that will count most to Theo.'

'Yes,' she agreed huskily, taking another deep breath before adding, 'He usually takes a nap after lunch. If you come at four o'clock, we'll tell him then.'

'Thank you.'

She gave him a wobbly smile. 'If that's everything settled, we should go back to the wedding reception. We'll be missed. It is Cass's night and I want to be there for her.'

'And I for George.'

Their first deal was still in place. He had to wait until tomorrow before taking what he wanted with Christina, yet her hand was still in his and as he rose from the table, the temptation to draw her up from her seat and straight into his embrace was irresistible. She didn't try to break free but her free hand fluttered in agitation against his chest and there was a heart-piercing vulnerability in the eyes that met his.

He hated her fear. It made him feel even more wrong about what he'd taken from her in the past. He pressed a soft kiss on her forehead and murmured, 'I'll make it right, Christina. For you and for Theo.'

He gave her what he hoped was a reassuring smile as he released her, only retaining her hand, keeping that physical link for the walk back to the wedding reception, wanting her to feel secure with him.

Tonight belonged to Cassandra and George.

Tomorrow was his.

He could wait.

CHAPTER TEN

TINA waited until after their Greek relatives departed for the mainland so she could have a private chat to her mother about her connection to Ari. Everyone had still been revelling in Cass's wedding—such a wonderful family celebration. Amongst the happy comments were a few arch remarks about Ari's interest in her.

'He didn't have eyes for anyone else.'

'Never left your side all evening.'

'Such a charming man!'

'And so handsome!'

Tina had shrugged off the curiosity, discouraging it by refocussing the conversation on her sister's life. However, she saw the same curiosity in her mother's eyes, and when they were finally alone together, relaxing on the lounges by the swimming pool, watching Theo practice diving into it, she didn't have to think about how to lead into revealing the truth. Her mother did it for her.

'Are you seeing Ari again today, Tina?'

'Yes. And there's something I have to tell you, Mama.' She took a deep breath to calm her jumpy nerves and started at the beginning. 'Ari Zavros and I were not meeting for the first time in Athens. Six years ago he was in Australia on a three-month tour of the wineries in our country. I met him on a modelling assignment and fell in love with him.'

Her mother instantly leapt to the truth, understanding of Ari's behaviour towards them flashing straight into her eyes. 'He's Theo's father.'

'Yes. I didn't expect to ever see him again. It was a shock when he was presented to us as George's best man. I asked him to wait until after the wedding before revealing that my son was also his because it would have been a major distraction from Cass and that wasn't fair, but today we have to deal with it, Mama.'

'Oh, my dear!' Her mother swung her legs off the lounge to face her directly with a look of anxious concern. 'These past few days must have been very difficult for you.'

Tina had to fight back tears. She hadn't expected such a rush of sympathy from her mother. Shock and perhaps criticism for her silence, worry over the situation, fretting over the choices to be made… she'd geared herself to cope with all this but not the caring for her feelings and the quick understanding of the distress she had been hiding.

'I thought…he was gone from my life, Mama,' she choked out. 'But he's not and he never will be again. He's made that very clear.'

'Yes…very clear,' her mother repeated, nodding as she recollected how Ari had inserted himself and his family into their time on Santorini. 'I don't think that's going to change, Tina. He's definitely intent on making a claim on his son.'

'And he has the wealth and power to back it up. There's no point in trying to resist his claim, Mama. I have to give way.'

'Has he said how he wants to deal with the situation?'

Tina's mouth instantly twisted into an ironic grimace. 'He wants me to marry him.'

'Ah!'

There was no real shock in that *Ah!*—more a realisation of the bigger claim being made—one that would completely change her daughter's life, as well as her grandson's.

After a few moments' thought, her mother asked, 'His family knows all this?'

'He told them after our meeting in Athens. He had no doubt that Theo was his child. His age…his eyes…'

'Yes…now I see.' Her mother nodded a few times. 'They have been extending a welcome to join their family because of Theo.'

'He is the main attraction,' Tina said dryly.

'But they have been very gracious to us, as well, Tina. Which shows they are prepared to accept you as Ari's wife. How do you feel about it?'

She shook her head. 'I don't know. He said he would have come back to me had I told him he'd left me pregnant. I didn't tell him because he didn't love me. I was only a…a charming episode…that he could walk away from.'

'But you loved him.'

'Yes. Totally.'

'And now?'

'I doubt there will ever be anyone else for me, Mama, but it's Theo he wants. I can't fool myself that I'm suddenly the woman he loves above all others.'

'Perhaps you are more special to him now because you are the mother of his child. It's a very Greek way of thinking, Tina. And sometimes love grows from sharing the most precious things to both of you.'

Tina choked up, remembering Ari listing how much he had missed of Theo because she had denied him knowledge of his son.

Her mother heaved a sigh. 'It's not for me to say what you should do, my darling. What do you think is best for you?'

'Oh, probably to marry him,' Tina said in a rush, relieved in a way to finally have it out in the open. 'I think he will be a good father. He's asked me to wait until he comes here this afternoon for us to tell Theo together that he does have a Papa. And after that—well, Ari and I need some time alone to…to see how we feel about each other, Mama. He wants to take me somewhere. Will you look after Theo, have him in your room tonight?'

'Oh, dear!' Her mother shook her head in dismay at realising what the all-night arrangement most probably meant. 'There's so much to take in. I wish your father was here.'

'Don't worry, Mama. I have to make a decision and I think this is the best way to do it.'

'Well, of course I will look after Theo, but…do be careful, Tina,' she said anxiously. 'If you decide not to marry Ari…I remember how you were when you were pregnant with Theo.'

'That won't happen again, Mama,' Tina assured her. It didn't matter this time if Ari used a contraceptive or not. She knew she was in a safe period of her cycle. She reached across and took her mother's hand. 'Thank you taking all this so well. I hate being a problem to you.'

'Not a problem, dear. Just… I do so want you to have a happy life and I wish with all my heart that everything turns out well with Ari.'

The fairy-tale happy ending.

Maybe if she could believe in it enough, it might happen. She'd have a better idea of how the future would run after tonight. Right now she couldn't trust Ari's word that he would remain a faithful husband. Even if they did find sexual pleasure with each other, that was no guarantee he would always be satisfied with her. She might begin to believe they really could forge a good marriage together after he signed the prenuptial agreement.

If he did.

Ari spent an extremely vexatious morning with his lawyer who was dead against signing away paternal rights under any circumstances. A financial settlement was fine in the case of divorce but giving up one's children was utter madness, especially since Ari was marrying to have his son.

'I'm not here for your advice,' Ari had finally said. 'Just draw up the agreement I've spelled out to you. It's an issue of showing good faith and I *will* show it.'

'Show it by all means,' his lawyer shot back at it him, 'but don't sign it.'

He hadn't…yet.

He'd done many deals in his life but none as risky as the one he'd proposed to Christina. The money didn't worry him. He would never begrudge financial support for her and their children. But if the response he needed from her was not forthcoming tonight, marrying her might be too much of a gamble.

His head told him this.

Yet his heart was already set on having Christina Savalas as his wife.

She touched him in ways no other woman had. He had been her first lover, almost certainly her only one, which made her his in a very primal sense. Plus the fact she had carried his child made her uniquely special. Besides, his wealth was not a big attraction to her or she would have gone after a slice of it to support their son rather than taking complete responsibility for him. She was only concerned about the kind of person he was. Looks, money…none of that counted. If he didn't measure up as a man she wanted in her life, he'd be out of it.

He'd never been challenged like this. Who he was on the surface of it had always been enough. Christina was hitting him at deeper levels and he felt totally driven to prove he did measure up—driven to remove all fear from her eyes. Winning her over had somehow become more important than anything else in his life.

The compelling tug of having Theo was a big part of it, but she was part of Theo, too. Ari couldn't separate them in his mind. Didn't want to separate them. The three of them made a family. *His* family. He had to make it so by any means possible because he couldn't tolerate the idea of Christina taking their son back to Australia and shutting him out of their lives as much as she legally could.

He lunched with his parents who were eager for another visit with their grandson. 'Tomorrow,' Ari promised them. 'I'll bring Christina and Theo and Helen back here tomorrow to sort out what is to be done.'

He had to stop them leaving Santorini on schedule. Even if Christina rejected his offer of marriage, she had to see reason about discussing future arrangements for their son. If she accepted his proposal, they would have a wedding to plan. More than a wedding. There would be many decisions to be made on setting up a life together—tying up ends in Australia, where best to make their home.

Ari was tense with determination as he drove to the El Greco resort. He told himself the meeting with Theo was relatively uncomplicated. There was no need to be uptight about his son's response. He had wished for a Papa. Revealing who that Papa was would certainly be a pleasure. What happened afterwards with Christina was the critical time. He fiercely hoped that was going to be a pleasure, too. If it wasn't… He instantly clicked his mind off any negative train of thought. This had to work.

Tina and her mother and Theo were sitting at one of the snack bar tables having afternoon tea when Ari arrived. He came striding down the ramp to the pool patio, a hard purposeful expression on his face, and headed straight towards where their rooms were located.

'We're here!' Tina called out, rising from her chair to catch his attention, her heartbeat instantly accelerating at what his arrival meant for both her and Theo.

His head jerked around and his expression immediately lightened on seeing them. Theo jumped off his chair and ran to meet him. Ari scooped him up in his arms and perched him against his shoulder, smiling broadly at his son's eagerness to welcome him.

'I finished the train station. You must come and see it, Ari,' Theo prattled happily.

'As soon as I say hello to your mother and grandmother,' he promised.

He shot a sharp look of enquiry at Tina as he approached their table. She nodded, assuring him her mother had been told. He smiled at both of them but the smile didn't quite reach his eyes. It made Tina wonder how tense he was over the situation. Marriage was a big step and it might not be the best course for them to take. Was he having second thoughts about his proposal?

He addressed her mother directly, speaking in a quiet tone that carried an impressive intensity of purpose. 'Helen, I want you to know I will look after your daughter with much more care than I did in the past. Please trust me on that.'

'Tina and Theo are very precious to me, Ari,' her mother answered. 'I hope your caring will be as deep as mine.'

He nodded and turned his gaze to Tina. 'Theo wants me to see his train station.'

'I'll take you to our room. He did a great job putting all the Lego together.' She smiled at her son. 'It was very tricky, wasn't it, darling?'

'Very tricky,' he echoed, then grinned triumphantly at Ari. 'But I did it!'

'I knew you were a clever boy,' he warmly approved.

'Will you wait here, Mama?' Tina asked.

'Yes, dear. Go on now.'

Theo was full of questions about Ari's nephews whom he'd spent most of his time with at the wedding reception. Tina didn't have to say anything on their walk to her room. She was acutely conscious of the easy bond Ari had already established with their son and felt fairly sure there would be no trauma attached to revealing the truth. If she made it like a fairy-tale to Theo, he might accept it unquestioningly. On the other hand, there could be a host of questions both of them would have to answer.

Her chest ached with tension as she opened the door to her room and stood aside for Ari to carry Theo inside. He paused a moment, giving her a burning look of command as he said, '*I'll* tell him.'

She felt an instant wave of resentment at his arbitrary taking over from her, yet it did relieve her of the responsibility of explaining the situation to Theo. *Let him get it right for their son,* she thought, closing the door behind them, then parking herself on the chair at the writing desk while Ari duly admired the Lego train station.

'Does your Mama tell you bed-time stories, Theo?' he asked, sitting down on the bed beside the fully con-structed station.

'Yes. She points to the words in the book and I can read some of them now,' he answered proudly.

'I think you must be very quick at learning things. If I tell you a story, I wonder if you could guess the end-ing,' Ari said with a teasing smile.

'Tell me! Tell me!' Theo cried eagerly, sitting cross-legged on the floor in front of Ari, his little body bent forward attentively.

Ari bent forwards, too, his forearms resting on his knees, his gaze locked on the amber eyes shining up at him. 'Once upon a time a prince from a faraway coun-try travelled to a land on the other side of the world.'

Tina was totally stunned that Ari had chosen to use a fairy story to convey the truth, yet how much of the truth would he tell? The tension inside her screwed up several notches.

'There he met a beautiful princess and she was like no one else he'd ever met. He wanted to be with her all the time and she wanted to be with him so they were together while he was in her country. But eventually he had to leave to carry out business for his kingdom back home. It hurt the princess very much when he said goodbye to her and when she found out that she was going to have a baby she decided not to send any message to the prince about it. She didn't want him to come back, then leave her again because it would hurt too much. So she kept the baby a secret from him.'

'Was the baby a boy or a girl?' Theo asked.

'It was a boy. And he was very much loved by her family. This made the princess think he didn't need a Papa because he already had enough people to love him. She didn't know that the boy secretly wished for a Papa.'

'Like me,' Theo popped in. 'But I didn't wish for one until I went to school. It was because my friends there have fathers.'

'It is only natural for you to want one,' Ari assured him.

'Does the boy in the story get his?'

'Let me tell you how it happened. After a few years the sister of the princess was to marry a man who came from the same country as the prince, so her family had to travel halfway around the world to attend the wedding. The princess didn't know that this man was a cousin of the prince and she would meet him again. It was a shock to her when she did, and when the prince saw her son, he knew the boy was his son, too. They had the same eyes.'

'Like you and me,' Theo said, instantly grasping the point.

'Yes. Exactly like that. But the princess asked the prince to keep her secret until after her sister's wedding because she didn't want to take people's attention away from the bride. The prince understood this but he wanted to spend as much time as he could with his son. And he also wanted the princess to know that being a father meant a lot to him. It made him very sad that he had missed out on so much of his son's life and he wanted to be there for him in the future.'

'Can I guess now?' Theo asked.

Ari nodded.

Theo cocked his head to the side, not quite sure he had it right, but wanting to know. 'Are you my Papa, Ari?'

'Yes, Theo. I am,' he answered simply.

Tina held her breath until she saw a happy grin break out on Theo's face. The same grin spread across Ari's. Neither of them looked at her. This was their moment—five years in the waiting—and she couldn't resent being excluded from it. It was her fault they had been kept apart all this time. Ari had been fair in his story-telling and she now had to be fair to the bond she had denied both of them.

'I'm glad you're my Papa,' Theo said fervently, rising to his feet. 'After my birthday party I dreamed that you were.'

Ari lifted him onto his knee, hugging him close. 'We'll always celebrate your birthday together,' he promised huskily.

'But I don't want you to hurt Mama again.'

Tears pricked Tina's eyes, her heart swelling at the love and loyalty in Theo's plea to his father.

'I am trying very hard not to,' Ari said seriously. 'I kept her secret until today, and now your Mama and I are going to work out how best we can be together for the rest of our lives. Will you be happy to be with your grandmother while we do that?'

'Does Yiayia know you're my Papa?'

'Yes. Your Mama told her this morning. And now that you know, too, you can talk about it to your grandmother. Tomorrow, if it's okay with your Mama, I'll take you to visit your other grandparents whom you met at your birthday party.'

Theo's eyes rounded in wonderment. 'Is Maximus my Papou?'

'Yes, and he very much wants to see you again. So does my mother. You will have a much bigger family. The boys you played with at the wedding are your cousins.'

'Will they be there tomorrow?'

'Yes.' Ari rose to his feet, hoisting Theo up in his arms. 'Let's go back to your grandmother because your Mama and I need to have some time to talk about all this.'

The face Theo turned to Tina was full of excitement. 'Is it okay with you, Mama?' he asked eagerly.

'Yes,' she said, not yet ready to commit to a mass family involvement until after her night with Ari, but smiling at her son to remove any worry from his mind.

It was enough for Theo.

He was content to be left with her mother, happy to share the news that his birthday wish had come true and ask a million questions about what might happen next. He waved goodbye to Tina and Ari without a qualm.

All the qualms were in Tina's stomach.

She was about to face a new beginning with Ari Zavros or an end to the idea of marrying him.

CHAPTER ELEVEN

Ari took her hand as they walked up the ramp to the courtyard in front of the reception building. The physical link flooded her mind with thoughts of the intimacy to come. For him it was probably just another night of sex—the performance of an act that had been commonplace in his life, varied only by the different women he'd taken to bed with him.

For her…a little shiver ran down her spine…it had been so long, and she wasn't dazzled by him this time.

Could she really shut off her disillusionment with the love she'd believed he'd shared and take pleasure in what he could give her? He'd said he'd try very hard not to hurt her. There was no need to be frightened of him, but she was frightened of the feelings he might evoke in her. This was not a time to be weak or confused. There was too much at stake to blindly follow instincts that had led her astray in the past.

Though she had to concede that Ari had been very good with Theo. He'd also saved her from the dilemma of how to explain the truth to their son. At least that was done with, and done well, which was only fair to acknowledge.

'I liked your fairy story,' she said, slanting him an appreciative little smile.

He flashed a hopeful smile back. 'We have yet to give it a happy ending.'

'To dream the impossible dream...' tripped straight off her tongue.

'Not impossible, Christina. Open your mind to it.'

They reached his car and he opened the passenger door for her. She paused, looking directly at him before stepping in. 'I don't know *your* mind, Ari. That's the problem.'

Intensity of purpose glittered in his amber eyes as he answered, 'Then I hope you'll know it better by tomorrow morning.'

'I hope I do, too.' She gestured to the car. 'Where are you taking me?'

'To Oia, the northern village of Santorini, the best place for watching the sunset. I've arranged for a suite in a boutique hotel which will give us the perfect view. I thought you would like it.'

'That's...very romantic.'

'With you I want to be romantic,' he replied, his whole expression softening with a look of rueful tenderness that twisted her heart.

She tore her gaze from his and quickly settled herself in the passenger seat, silently and furiously chastising herself for the craven wish to be romanced out of all her mistrust of his fairy-tale happy ending. He was going to make it all too easy to surrender to his charm and there was a huge vulnerable part of her that wanted to believe she was special to him this time and there would be no turning away from her ever again.

But it was his child he really wanted. She was the package deal. And she had no idea how long the package would stay attractive to him. Even if Ari romanced her beautifully tonight, she had to keep her head on straight and insist on the prenuptial agreement he'd offered. It was her insurance against making another big mistake with him.

He chatted to her about the various features of the island they passed on their way to Oia, intent on establishing a companionable mood. Tina did her best to relax and respond in an interested fashion. She remembered how interested he had been in Australia, always asking her questions about it whenever they were driving somewhere together.

'Where would you want us to live if I marry you, Ari?' she asked, needing to know what he had in mind.

He hesitated, then bluntly answered, 'Australia is too far away from my family's business interests, Christina. We could base ourselves anywhere in Europe. Athens if you would like to be near your relatives. Perhaps Helen would like to return there. She would see more of Cassandra and George in the future if she did, and put her closer to us, as well.'

It meant completely uprooting herself. And Theo. Though Ari had made a good point about her mother. So much change…she would end up leading an international life like Cass. Her sister had acclimatised herself to it. Loved it. Perhaps she would learn to love it, too.

'It's also a matter of choosing what might be best for our children's education,' Ari added, shooting her a quick smile.

Our children... It was a very seductive phrase. She adored having Theo. She'd love to have a little girl, as well. If she didn't marry Ari, it was highly unlikely that she would have any more children. But if she had them with Ari, she didn't want to lose them to him.

'Are you okay with that, Christina?' he asked, frowning at her silence.

'I'm opening my mind to it,' she tossed at him.

He laughed, delighted that it wasn't a negative answer.

They had to leave the car on the outskirts of the village and continue on foot through the narrow alleys to the hotel. Both of them had brought light backpacks with essentials for an overnight stay. It only took a minute to load them onto their shoulders and Ari once again took possession of Tina's hand for the walk into the village. It felt more comfortable now, especially as they navigated past the steady stream of tourists that thronged the alleys lined with fascinating shops.

Again she was acutely aware of women looking Ari over but the handhold meant he belonged to her, and she firmly reminded herself that not even Cass's beautiful model friends had turned his head last night. If she could just feel more confident that he could be content with only having her, the female attention he invariably drew might not worry her so much. It hadn't worried her in the past. She had been totally confident that he was hers. Until he wasn't hers any more.

But marriage was different to a *charming episode.*

A wedding ring on Ari's finger would make him legally hers.

Very publicly hers.

That should give her some sense of security with him.

In fact, being the wife of Ari Zavros would empower her quite a bit on many levels.

If she could make herself hard-headed enough to set aside any possible hurt from him in the future and simply go through with the marriage, dealing with each day as it came, her life could become far more colourful than she would ever manage on her own. Besides which if it ended in divorce, the financial settlement would give her the means to do whatever she chose. Wanting Ari to love her…well, that was probably wishing for the moon, but who knew? Even that might come to pass if her mother was right about sharing what was precious to both of them.

All the buildings in Oia were crammed up against each other, using every available bit of space. The entrance to the hotel opened straight onto an alley with pot-plants on either side of the door its only adornment. It was certainly boutique size. The man at the reception desk greeted Ari enthusiastically and escorted them to a suite on what proved to be the top level of three built down the hillside facing the sea. The bathroom, bedroom and balcony were all small but perfectly adequate and the view from the balcony was spectacular.

'Sunset is at eight o'clock,' their escort informed them before departing.

Almost three hours before then, Tina thought, dumping her backpack on a chair and gravitating straight to the balcony, suddenly too nervous to face Ari in the bedroom. A spiral staircase ran down the side of the hotel, linked by landings to each balcony, giving guests easy access to the small swimming pool which took up half the courtyard that extended from the hotel's lowest level. A few people were lounging on deck chairs beside it. She stared down at them, wondering where they had come from and what had brought them here. Probably nothing as complicated as her own situation.

Behind her she heard the pop of a champagne cork. A few moments later Ari was at her side carrying two glasses fizzing with the bubbly wine.

'You used to drink this with me. Will you try it again, Christina? It might relax you,' he said kindly.

She heaved a sigh to ease the tightness in her chest and took the glass he offered. 'Thank you. It's been six years since I was in an intimate situation with a man,' she said with a rueful smile. 'This might take the edge off.'

'I guess having Theo made it difficult for you to form relationships,' he remarked sympathetically.

Not Theo. You. But telling him so would let him know she was stuck on him and it was better that he didn't know. She didn't want him taking anything for granted where she was concerned.

'Don't worry that I'll make you pregnant tonight. I'll be very careful,' he assured her.

She shook her head. 'You won't anyway. This is a safe week for me.'

'Ah!' He grinned, the amber eyes twinkling with pleasure. 'Then we may be totally carefree which will be much better.' He clinked her glass with his. 'To a night of re-discovery, Christina.'

She took a quick sip of the champagne, hoping to settle the flock of butterflies in her stomach. Ari's arm slid around her waist, his hand resting warmly on the curve of her hip, bringing his body closer to hers, stirring memories of how well they had fitted together in the past and triggering the desire to re-discover every sweet nuance of her sexuality.

'I don't want to wait until tonight,' she said decisively, setting her glass down on the top of the balcony wall and turning to face him, a wave of reckless belligerence seizing her and pouring into urgent words. 'Let's just do it, Ari. I don't want to be romanced or seduced or…or treated to any other lover routine you've got. This is a need to know thing, isn't it?'

He set his glass down next to hers and scooped her hard against him, his freed hand lifting to her chin, tilting it up, his eyes blazing a heart-kicking challenge right at her. 'A great many needs to be answered on both sides and I don't want to wait, either.'

His mouth came down on hers so hard she jerked her head back, afraid of what she had just invited. He'd been a tender lover to her, never rough. Panic kicked into her heart. What did she know of him now? If he had no real feeling for her…

'Damn!' he muttered, his chest heaving as he sucked in breath, a glint of anguish in the eyes that bored into hers. 'I *will* control myself. Let me start again, Christina.'

He didn't wait for a reply. His lips brushed lightly over hers, back and forth, back and forth, making them tingle to the point where she welcomed the running of his tongue-tip over them. *Yes,* she thought dizzily, the stiffness melting from her body, panic washed away by a soothing flood of warmth. She lifted her arms and wound them around his neck as she gave herself up to a kiss that was more familiar to her, a loving kind of kiss.

She didn't mind opening her mouth to the gentle probe of his tongue, liking the intimate sensation of tangling her own with it, the slow gathering of excitement. It was easy to close her eyes and forget the years of nothing, remembering only the girl she had been in this man's arms, experiencing sexual pleasure for the first time.

His hand slid down over her bottom, pressing her closer to him, and the hardness of his erection filled her mind with giddy elation. He couldn't fake that. He really did want her. She was still desirable to him so it was okay to desire him, too. And she did, quite fiercely, given the confidence that this wasn't just a cynical seduction to weaken her stance against him.

A wild ripple of exultation shot through her when his kissing took on a more passionate intensity, his tongue driving deep, challenging her to meet its thrust, revel in the explosion of need behind it. Her hands slid into his hair, fingers digging in hard to hold his head to hers, the desire to take possession of him and keep him forever running rampant through her mind.

He couldn't walk away from this.

Not ever again.

She wouldn't let him.

He wrenched his head from her tight grasp, lifting it back from her mouth enough to gasp, 'Must move from here. Come.'

He scooped her off the balcony and into the bedroom, striding for the bed with her firmly tucked to his side. Tina's heart was pounding with both fear and excitement. This was the moment to undress. She would see him again fully naked. But he would see her, too. How did she measure up against the other women who'd been in his life... the blonde in Dubai whose breasts had been more voluptuous?

But he *was* aroused, so maybe the *idea* of her made physical factors irrelevant. And although she was carrying more flesh than when he had been with her before, her body was still okay—no looseness from having the baby. It was silly to fret over it. He wanted sex with her. He was up and ready for it and it was going to happen.

He stopped close to the bed and swung her to face him, his hands curling around her shoulders, his eyes sweeping hers for any hint of last-minute rejection. She stared back steadily, determined not to baulk at this point.

'You move me as no other woman ever has, Christina,' he murmured, and planted a soft warm kiss on her forehead.

Her heart contracted at those words. Whether they

were true or not, the wish to believe them was too strong to fight. She closed her eyes wanting to privately hug the strong impression of sincerity in his, and he gently kissed her eyelids, sealing the positive flow of feeling he had evoked.

She felt his thumbs hook under the straps of the green sundress she'd worn and slowly slide them down her upper arms. He kissed her bared shoulders as he un-zipped the back of her bodice. Tina kept her eyes shut, fiercely focussing on her other senses, loving the soft brush of his lips against her skin and the gentle caress of his fingers along her spine as it, too, was bared. She breathed in the slightly spicy scent of his cologne. It was the same as when they were together before. He hadn't changed it. And the thrill of his touch was the same, too.

Her dress slithered down to the floor. The style of it hadn't required a bra so now her breasts were naked. Her only remaining garment was her green bikini pants, but he didn't set about removing this last piece of cloth-ing. His hands cupped her breasts, stroking them with a kind of reverence that she found emotionally confusing until he asked, 'Did you breast-feed Theo, Christina?'

He was thinking of his son. He was not looking at her as a woman but as the mother of his child.

'Yes,' she answered huskily, telling herself it was okay for him to see her in this light. It made her dif-ferent to the other women who'd been in his life. More special. Her body had carried his child, had nurtured his child.

'He must have been a very happy baby,' he murmured, and his mouth enclosed one of her nipples, his tongue swirling around it before he sucked on it.

Tina gasped at the arc of piercing pleasure that hit her stomach and shot past it to the apex of her thighs. Her hands flew up and grasped his shoulders, fingers digging into his muscles, needing something strong to hold onto as quivers ran through her entire body. He moved his mouth to her other breast, increasing the sweet turbulence inside her. For her it had been a physical pleasure breast-feeding Theo but it hadn't generated this acute level of sexual excitement. Tina was so wound up in it, she didn't know if it was a relief or a disappointment when he lifted his head away.

Almost immediately he was whipping down her bikini pants and her feet automatically stepped out of them. Any concern about how she looked to him had completely disappeared. He scooped her into such a crushing embrace she could feel his heart thumping against his chest-wall and then he was kissing her again; hard, hungry kisses that sparked an overwhelming hunger for him. She wanted this man. She'd never stopped wanting him.

He lifted her off her feet and laid her on the bed. The sudden loss of contact with him instantly opened her eyes. He was discarding his clothes with such haste Tina was in no doubt of his eagerness to join her, and it was thrilling to watch his nakedness emerge. He was a truly beautiful man with a perfect male body. His olive skin gleamed over well-defined muscles. His smooth hairless chest was sculpted for touching, for gliding hands over it. He had the lean hips and powerful thighs of a top athlete. And there was certainly no doubt about his desire for her, his magnificent manhood flagrantly erect.

Yet when he came to her he ignored any urgency for instant sexual satisfaction. He lay beside her, one arm sliding under her shoulders to draw her into full body contact with him, his free hand stroking long, lovely caresses as his mouth claimed hers again, more in a slow seductive tasting than greedy passion. It gave her the freedom to touch him, to revel in feeling his strong masculinity against her softer femininity, the whole wonderfully sensual intimacy of flesh against flesh.

His hand dipped into the crevice between her thighs, his fingers moving gently, back and forth, intent on building excitement until she felt the exquisite urgency he had always made her feel in the past. Tina lifted her leg over his, giving him easier access to her, refusing to let any inhibitions deny her the pleasure she remembered. He changed the nature of his kissing, his tongue thrusting and withdrawing, mimicking the rhythm of what was to come, accelerating the need to have him there.

But still he didn't hurry. He moved down the bed, trailing kisses to the hollow of her throat, then sucking briefly on her breasts, heightening their sensitivity before sliding his mouth to her stomach, running his tongue around her navel.

'Was it a difficult labour with Theo, Christina?' he asked in a deeply caring tone.

She'd been so focussed on feeling, it took a concentrated effort to find her voice. 'Some…some hard hours,' she answered, savagely wishing he wasn't thinking of their son. Yet that was why he was here, with her, doing what he was doing, and she wouldn't be having this if she hadn't had his child.

'I should have been there,' he murmured, pressing his mouth to her stomach as though yearning for that lost time. 'I would have been there. And I will be for the rest of our children,' he said more fiercely before lifting himself further down to kiss her where his son had emerged from her womb.

I'm not going to think of why, Tina decided with wild determination. *I want this. I want him inside me again.*

The tension building in her body obliterated any further thought. Need was screaming through every nerve. It reached the point where she jack-knifed up to pluck at his shoulders, crying out, 'Enough! Enough!' She couldn't bear another second of waiting for him.

To her intense relief he responded instantly, surging up to fit himself between her legs which were already lifting to curl around his hips in a compulsive urging for the action she frantically craved. Her inner muscles were convulsing as he finally entered her and just one deep plunge drove her to an explosive climax, the exquisite torture peaking then melting into wave after wave of ecstatic pleasure as Ari continued the wonderfully intimate stroking.

It was incredibly satisfying, feeling him filling her again and again. Her body writhed exultantly around him. Her hands dragged up and down his back, urging on the rhythm of mutual possession. The sheer elation of it was so marvellously sweet nothing else existed for Tina, not the why or the where or the how.

When Ari cried out at his own climax, it sounded like a triumphant trumpet of joy to her ears. *She* had brought him to this. He shared the same heights of sensation he had led her to. And she revelled in that sense of intense togetherness as all his mighty strength collapsed on her and she hugged him with all her strength. He rolled onto his side, clutching her tightly against him, holding onto the deep connection, clearly wanting it to last as long as possible.

He didn't speak for quite a long time and Tina didn't want to break the silence. She lay with her head tucked under his chin, listening to his pulse-rate slowing to a normal beat. It was the first time today she actually felt totally relaxed. The sex-test was over. He had certainly satisfied her as a lover and if he was satisfied that she wouldn't turn her back on him, maybe they could move towards a commitment to each other.

It might even have a chance of sticking.

If she kept on having his children.

Was that the key to having him come to love her?

If only she could be sure he would in the end…truly love her for herself…and never want any other woman.

Marrying Ari was a terrible gamble.

But having had him again, she didn't want to let him go.

CHAPTER TWELVE

ARI felt happy. Usually after sex he felt satisfied, content, relaxed. Happiness was something more and it made him wonder if it was a temporary thing or whether having Christina would always give him this exultant sense of joy. Maybe it was simply a case of having risen to the challenge and won the response he wanted from her.

It had been damnably difficult to rein himself in to begin with. Having been forced to exercise control on the physical front for the past few days and suddenly being presented with the green light to go ahead, all the bottled-up desire he'd felt had blown his mind. And almost blown his chance with her.

But she wasn't pulling away from him now. He wished she still had long hair. He remembered how much he'd enjoyed running his fingers through it when she'd lain with him like this in the past. Though it didn't really matter. It was so good just having her content to stay where she was—no barriers between them. No *physical* barriers. He hoped the mental resistance she'd had to him had been stripped away, too.

He knew he'd given her intense sexual pleasure. Was it enough to sway her into marrying him? She had to be considering what Theo wanted in his life, too, and there was no doubt he wanted his father. What more could be done to clinch a future together?

He probably should be talking to her, finding out what was in her mind, yet he was reluctant to break the intimate silence. They had all night, plenty of time for talking. It was great being able to revel in the certainty that she would not be cold to him in the marriage bed.

She stirred, lifting her head. 'I need to go to the bathroom, Ari.'

He released her and she instantly rolled away and onto her feet on the other side of the bed, only giving him a back view of her as she walked swiftly to the bathroom, no glimpse of the expression on her face. However, he couldn't help smiling at the lovely curve of her spine, the perkiness of her sexy bottom and the perfect shape of her long legs.

There was nothing unattractive about Christina Savalas. No one would be surprised at his choice of wife. Not that he cared about what anyone else thought but it would make it easier for Christina to be readily accepted as his partner in life. Women could be quite bitchy if they perceived any other woman as not measuring up to what they expected. Felicity Fulbright had sniped about quite a few while in his company.

Of course he would be on guard to protect Christina from any nastiness but there were always female get-togethers when he wouldn't be present. On the other hand, the fighting spirit his father admired in her was undoubtedly a force to be reckoned with in any kind of critical situation. She would have no qualms about setting people straight as she saw it. She'd done it to him repeatedly in the past few days.

All in all, Ari was quite looking forward to a future with Christina now that the sexual question was answered. However, his satisfaction took a slight knock when she re-emerged from the bathroom, wearing a white cotton kimono which covered her from neck to ankle. It signalled that she wasn't about to jump back into bed with him.

'I found this hanging on a peg behind the bathroom door,' she said, putting a firm knot in the tie-belt and not quite meeting his gaze as she added, 'There's another one for you if you want to wear it after your shower. Easier than re-dressing for sitting on the balcony to watch the sunset.'

And easier for undressing afterwards, Ari thought, accepting her plan of action without argument. It was obvious that she had already showered—no invitation for him to join her—so she was putting an end to their intimacy for a while, which raised questions about how eager she was to continue it. An intriguing combination—hot in bed, cool out of it—another challenge that he had to come to grips with.

She wasn't won yet.

'Have a look at the menu on the desk while I shower,' he said invitingly. 'See what you'd like for dinner. We can order it in.'

It stopped her stroll towards the balcony. She paused at the desk to pick up the menu and began to study it, not even glancing at him as he rose from the bed and moved towards the bathroom. Was she embarrassed by her body's response to his love-making? Was she always going to close up on him afterwards? How much was she truly willing to share with him?

Ari mused over these questions while taking a shower. In every one of his relationships with women there had always been mutual desire and mutual liking, at least at the beginning. It had certainly been so with Christina six years ago. In fact, looking back, that had been the only relationship he'd been reluctant to end. Nothing had soured it. Christina had not deceived him in any way, nor done anything to turn him off. The timing had been wrong, nothing else.

He was still sure his reasons for limiting it to his time in Australia were valid, yet his decision then kept coming between them now and he was no longer sure that good sex was the answer to reaching the kind of relationship he wanted with his wife.

Though it still made the marriage viable.

The mutual desire was right.

He just had to work on getting the mutual liking right again.

Having picked up their clothes from the floor and hung them over a chair, Tina took the menu out to the balcony and sat down at the small table for two. She was hungry, having only had a very light lunch, too full of nervous tension to enjoy food. Now that she felt less uptight about spending the night with Ari, a sunset dinner was very appealing.

She studied the list of dishes with interest, thinking this was the first meal she would spend alone with Ari since meeting him again. It was an opportunity to extend her knowledge of his lifestyle, which was an important preparation for being his wife. There was more to marriage than good sex and she wasn't about to let Ari think that was all he had to give her.

Though it was a very powerful drawcard, completely meddling with Tina's common sense when he strolled out to the balcony. His white kimono barely reached his knees and left a deep V of gleaming olive-skinned chest, causing her to catch her breath. He was so overwhelmingly male and so vitally handsome, all her female hormones were zinging as though caught in an electrical storm. Chemistry still humming from the sex they'd just shared, Tina told herself, but the desire for more of it could not be denied.

'Found what you'd like?' he asked, gesturing towards the menu.

'Yes.' She rattled off a starter, a main dish, and sweets, as well.

He grinned approval at her. 'I've worked up an appetite, too. Give me the menu and I'll call in an order now.' He nodded at the lowering sun. 'It will be pleasant to dine as we watch the sunset.'

Both the sky and the sea were already changing colour. Ari tucked the menu under his arm, picked up the half-empty champagne glasses from the balcony wall and returned to the bedroom to make the call. Tina watched the shimmering waves with their shifting shades of light, trying to calm herself enough to conduct a normal conversation without being continually distracted by lustful thoughts.

Ari brought back two clean wine glasses and an ice-bucket containing a bottle of light white wine which he said would go well with their starters. Tina decided she might as well give up her alcohol ban. Wine was part and parcel of Ari's life and it was more appropriate for his wife to partake of some of it.

He was standing by the balcony wall, opening the bottle of wine when he was hailed from below.

'Ari... Ari... It is you, isn't it?'

Tina's nerves instantly twanged. It was a female voice with a very British accent, like that of the woman who'd been with him in Dubai.

He looked down, his shoulders stiffening as he recognised the person. He raised a hand in acknowledgement but made no vocal reply, quickly turning back to the task of filling their glasses. His mouth had thinned into a line of vexation. His eyes were hooded.

Clearly this was an unwelcome intrusion and Tina felt impelled to ask, 'Who is it?' Facing other women who'd been in his life would have to be done sooner or later and it was probably better that she had a taste of it now, know whether or not she could deal with it.

He grimaced. 'Stephanie Gilchrist. A London socialite.'

'Not a fond memory?' she queried archly, pretending it wasn't important.

His eyes blazed annoyance. 'An acquaintance. No more. I see she's here with her current playmate, Hans

Vogel, a German model who's always strutting his stuff. I had no idea they were booked into this hotel.'

Just two people he didn't want to mix with tonight, Tina thought with considerable relief. She didn't really want to be faced with a woman who had shared his bed, not when the intimacies they had just shared were so fresh in her mind, not when her body was still reacting to them. This new beginning would not feel so good. Later on, when she felt more confident about being Ari's partner—when he made her feel more confident—it might not matter at all.

'Ari!' Stephanie called more demandingly.

'Damned nuisance!' he muttered savagely as he swung around to deal with the problem.

Having regained his attention, Stephanie bluntly asked, 'What are you doing here? I thought you had a home on Santorini. I'm sure Felicity told me...'

'This hotel has a better view of the sunset,' Ari swiftly cut in. 'Why don't you and Hans just lie back on your lounges and enjoy it?'

He waved his hand dismissively but Stephanie apparently had some personal axe to grind with him. 'I'm coming up,' she announced belligerently.

Ari cursed under his breath. He turned sharply to Tina, his brow creased with concern, the amber eyes glittering with intense urgency. 'I'm sorry. I can't stop her. The spiral staircase is open to all guests. I will get rid of her as fast as I can.'

Tina shrugged. 'I can be polite to one of your acquaintances for a few minutes,' she said, eyeing him warily, wondering if he had lied to her about the less than intimate connection to this woman.

Ari swiftly rattled out information. 'She's a close friend of Felicity Fullbright. Felicity was the woman you saw me with in Dubai. Since Stephanie is here, I don't know if she's been told I've ended the relationship with her friend. Anything she says… it's irrelevant to us, Christina. Don't let it worry you.'

It worried him.

Here's where I learn if I'm a fool to even consider marrying him, Tina thought, putting a steel guard around her vulnerability to this man.

Her heart started a painful pounding. 'How long were you with Felicity, Ari?' she asked, needing to know more.

'Six weeks. It was enough to decide she didn't suit me,' he answered tersely.

'You haven't been with me for a week yet,' she pointed out just as tersely.

The clip-clop of sandals was getting closer.

Ari frowned, shaking his head at her assertion. 'It's different with you, Christina.'

Because of Theo. But if they married, he would have to live with her, too, and how long would that suit him? They had had a harmonious relationship for three months but still he'd left her. It hadn't been enough to keep him at her side.

Stephanie's arrival on the staircase landing adjacent to their balcony put a halt to any further private conversation. She was a very curvy blonde with a mass of long, crinkly hair, and wearing a minute blue bikini that left little to the imagination. Her very light, almost aquamarine eyes instantly targeted Tina.

'Well, well, off with the old and on with the new,' she drawled. Her gaze shifted to Ari. 'That must be a quick-change record even for you. I ran into Felicity at Heathrow just a few days ago. She was flying in from Athens and Hans and I were on our way here. She said you'd split but she sure didn't know you had a replacement lined up.'

No waiting for an introduction.

No courtesy at all.

Tina sat tight, watching Ari handle the situation.

'You're assuming too much, Stephanie,' he said blandly, gesturing towards Tina. 'This is Christina Savalas whom I met in Australia quite a few years ago. She happens to be Cassandra's sister who married my cousin, George, yesterday. The wedding gave us the opportunity to catch up again, which has been amazingly good.' He smiled at Tina. 'Wouldn't you say?'

'Amazing,' she echoed, following his lead and smiling back at him.

Stephanie arched her eyebrows. 'Australia? Are you heading back there now that the wedding is over?'

Tina shrugged. 'I shall have to go sometime.'

'Not in any hurry since you've snagged Ari again,' came the mocking comment.

The woman's sheer rudeness goaded Tina into a very cold retort. 'I'm not into snagging men. In fact...'

'I'm the one doing all the running,' Ari cut in. 'And having found out what you wanted to know, why don't you run along back to Hans, Stephanie? You're not exactly endearing yourself to a woman I care about.'

'Really care?' She gave Ari a derisive sneer. 'It's not just a dose of the charm you used to bowl over Felicity? You didn't care about her one bit, did you?'

'Not after she displayed a dislike for children, no,' he answered bitingly.

'Oh!' With her spite somewhat deflated, she turned to Tina for a last jeer. 'Well, I've just done you a favour. You'd better show a liking for children or he'll throw you over as fast as he caught up with you. Good luck!'

With a toss of her hair she flounced off their balcony.

Tina stared out to sea as Stephanie's sandals clattered down the spiral staircase. She wondered if it was good luck or bad that had brought her back into Ari's life. Whatever…luck had little to do with making a marriage work. At least, a liking for children was one thing they definitely shared. Ari wouldn't be throwing her over on that issue. But Stephanie had implied he had a quick turnover of women in his life, which meant he wasn't in the habit of holding onto a relationship. What if she didn't *suit* him after a while?

'You hardly know me, Ari,' she said, suddenly frightened that her suitability might be very limited.

'I know enough to want you as my wife,' he whipped out, an emphatic intensity in his voice. 'And not only because you've given me a son. There's nothing I don't like about you, Christina.'

She sliced him a wary look. 'What do you actively *like?*'

He sat down at the table, pushing one of the glasses

of wine over to her, obviously playing for time to think. 'Take a sip. It doesn't have a sour taste like Stephanie,' he assured her.

She picked up the glass and sipped, eyeing him over its rim.

The expression on his face softened, the amber eyes telegraphing appreciation. 'I like how much you care for your family. I like the way you consider others. I like your good manners. I think you have courage and grit and intelligence—all qualities that I like. They make up the kind of character that I want in a partner.'

He wasn't talking love. He was ticking off boxes. She could tick off the same boxes about him. A match-making agency would probably place them as a likely couple, especially since there was no lack of sexual chemistry between them. But there was one big factor missing.

Tina heaved a sigh as she remembered how Cass and George had acted towards each other yesterday. It hurt that she would never have that wonderful emotional security with Ari. What if she married him and he was bowled over by some other woman further down the track? It could happen. She had to be prepared for it, safeguard herself against it, be practical about what she could expect from him and what she couldn't.

'Tell me about your life, Ari,' she said, needing to feel more informed about what a future with him would entail. 'What are the business interests that take you travelling? I only know of your connection to the wine industry.'

He visibly relaxed, happy to have the Stephanie can of worms closed.

Tina listened carefully to the list of property investments the Zavros family had made in many countries as far apart as Spain and Dubai where Ari had so recently been checking up on an estate development. Mostly they were connected to the tourist industry—resorts and theme parks and specialty shops. They had also tapped into the food industry with olives, cheeses and wine.

'You're in charge of all this?' she enquired.

He shook his head. 'My father runs the ship. I report and advise. The decisions are ultimately his. Most of the family is involved in one capacity or another.'

It was big business—far more complex than managing a restaurant. Tina continued to question him about it over dinner which was as tasty as it had promised to be. The sunset was gorgeous, spreading a rosy hue over all the white buildings on the hillside that faced it. For real lovers this had to be a very romantic place, Tina thought, but she couldn't feel it with Ari. As charming as he was, as good a lover as he was, no way could she bring herself to believe she was the light of his life.

Her own experience prompted her to ask, 'Have you ever been in love, Ari? So in love that person mattered more than anything else? Wildly, passionately, out of your mind...*in love?*'

As she'd been with him.

He frowned, obviously not liking the question. His jaw tightened as he swung his gaze away from hers, staring out to sea. She saw the corner of his mouth turn down into a grimace. He had experienced it, she thought, but not with her. A lead weight settled on her heart. He might very well experience it again with someone else.

CHAPTER THIRTEEN

IN LOVE...

Ari hated that memory. It was the one and only time he'd completely lost his head over a woman. He'd been her fool, slavishly besotted with her while she had only been amusing herself with him.

He wished Christina hadn't asked the question. Yet if he wasn't honest with her she would probably sense it and that would be a black mark against him in her mind. Besides, he was a different person to the boy he was then. He just didn't like dragging up that long-buried piece of the past and laying it out but he had to now. He'd left Christina too long without a reply.

He turned to her, the cynicism he'd learnt from that experience burning in his eyes and drawling through his voice. 'Wildly, passionately in love...yes, that happened to me when I was eighteen. She was very beautiful, exotically glamorous, and incredibly erotic. I would have done anything for her and did do everything she asked.'

'How long did it last?'

'A month.'

Christina raised her eyebrows. 'What made you fall out of love?'

'Being faced with reality.'

'Something you didn't like?'

'I hadn't understood what I was to her. I knew she was years older than me. It didn't matter. Nothing mattered but being with her. I thought she felt the same about me. It was so intense. But she was simply enjoying the intensity, revelling in her power to make me do whatever she wanted.'

'How did you come to realise that?'

'Because I was her Greek toy-boy, a last fling before she married her much more mature American millionaire. *It's been fun,* she said as she kissed me goodbye. *Fun...*'

He snarled the word and immediately cursed himself for letting it get to him after all these years.

'You were badly hurt,' Christina murmured sympathetically.

He shrugged. 'I'm not likely to fall in love again, if that's what you're worried about, Christina. Being someone's fool does not appeal to me.'

'You think your head will always rule your heart?'

'It has since I was eighteen.'

Except with her and Theo. His heart was very much engaged with his son and according to his lawyer, he'd completely lost his head in proposing the prenuptial agreement to induce Christina to marry him, ensuring that Theo would be a constant in his life. But he did feel the fidelity clause was not so much of a risk now. And he did like and admire Christina. He would make the marriage work. They would have more children... a family...

'I was eighteen when I fell in love with you.'

The quietly spoken words jolted Ari out of his confident mood and sent an instant chill down his spine. Her dark eyes were flat, expressionless, steadily watching whether he understood the parallel of what had been done to him—not only the hurt, the rejection of any lasting value in the love offered, but also the shadow it cast over any deep trust in a relationship. Giving oneself completely to another was not on. He'd never done it again.

Was this how Christina felt about him? Had he just ruined every bit of progress he'd made with her, bringing the past back instead of focussing her mind on the future they could have? Was this why he couldn't reach what he wanted to reach in her? He had to fix this. It was intolerable that she cast him in the same mould as the woman who'd taken him for a ride.

Before he could find the words to defend himself she spoke again, cocking her head to one side, her eyes alert to weighing up his reply. 'Did you think it was *fun* at the time?'

'Not like that!' he denied vehemently. He leaned towards her, gesturing an appeal for fairness. 'There was no one else in my life, Christina. I wasn't having a fling with you, cheating on a woman I intended to marry. The thought of having a little fun with you never crossed my mind. That was not part of it, I swear. I was enchanted by you.'

'For a while.' Her mouth twisted with irony. 'I can

imagine an older woman being enchanted by you when you were eighteen, Ari. You would have been absolutely beautiful. But her head ruled her heart, just as yours did with me. Too young…wasn't that how you explained leaving me behind?'

'You're not too young now.' The urgent need to stop this treacherous trawling through the past pushed Ari to his feet. He took Christina's hands, pulling her out of her chair and into his embrace, speaking with a violence of feeling that exploded off his tongue. 'I wanted you beyond any common sense then. And God knows I've lost any common sense since I've met you again. I want you so much it's been burning me up from the moment I saw you in Dubai. So forget everything else, Christina. Forget everything but this.'

He forgot about being gentle with her. The fierce emotion welling up in him demanded that he obliterate any bad thoughts from her mind and fill it with the same all-consuming desire he felt. He kissed her hard, storming her mouth with intense passion. A wild exultation ran through him as she responded with her own fierce drive to take what he was doing and give it right back.

No hesitation.

No holding back.

Frenzied kisses.

Frenzied touching.

Mutual desire riding high, her body pressed yearningly to his, making him even more on fire for her. Primitive instincts kicked in. He needed, wanted, had to have total possession of this woman. He swept her off her feet, crushed her to his chest as he strode to the bed. Even as he laid her down she was pushing her kimono apart, opening her legs wide for him, not wanting to wait, eagerly inviting instant intimacy.

He tore his own robe off, hating the thought of it getting in the way. Then he was with her, swiftly positioning himself. She was slick and hot, exciting him even further with her readiness. Her legs locked around him, heels digging into his buttocks, urging him on. He pushed in hard and fast and barely stopped himself from climaxing at the very first thrust, just like a teenage boy experiencing the ultimate sex fit.

He sucked in a quick breath, savagely telling himself to maintain control. He tried to set up a slow, voluptuous rhythm with his hips but she wouldn't have it, her body rocking his to go faster, faster. He felt her flesh clenching and unclenching around his and her throat emitted an incredibly sexy groan.

His head was spinning, excitement at an intense level. Her fingers dug into the nape of his neck. Her back arched from the bed. He felt the first spasm of her coming and was unable to hold off his own release any longer. He cried out as it burst from him in violent shudders, and the flood of heat from both of them was so ecstatically satisfying he was totally dazed by the depth of feeling.

He'd collapsed on top of her. She held him in a tightly possessive hug. Was she feeling the same? He had to know. Had to know if all the bad stuff from the past had been wiped out of her mind. He levered himself up on his elbows to see her face. Her eyes were closed, her head thrown back, her lips slightly apart, sucking in air and slowly releasing it.

'Look at me, Christina,' he gruffly commanded.

Her long lashes flicked up. Her eyes were dilated, out of focus. A thrill of triumph ran riot through Ari's mind. She was still feeling him inside her, revelling in the sheer depth of sensation. It gave him a surge of confidence that she wouldn't walk away from this— what they could have together. The glazed look slowly cleared. Her tongue slid out and licked her lips. He was tempted to flick his own tongue over them, but that would start them kissing again and this moment would be swallowed up and he wouldn't know what it meant to her.

'This is now, Christina,' he said with passionate fervour. 'The past is gone. This is now and you're feeling good with me. Tell me that you are.'

'Yes.' The word hissed out on a long sigh. She half-smiled as she added, 'I'm feeling good.'

He nodded. 'So am I. And I truly believe we can always make each other feel good if the will is there to do it.' He lifted a hand to stroke the soft black bangs of hair away from her forehead, his eyes boring into hers to enforce direct mental contact with her. 'We can be great partners in every sense there is, starting now, Christina. We look ahead, not back. Okay?'

There was no instant response but her eyes didn't disengage from his. Their focus sharpened and he had the feeling she was trying to search his soul. He had nothing to hide, yet he was acutely conscious of tension building inside him as he waited for her answer.

He'd hurt her in the past and she'd nursed that hurt for years. It had erupted in his face tonight and he was asking her to let it go, leave it behind them. It was a big ask. He recalled the look of heart-piercing vulnerability he'd seen after they'd made the sex-deal last night. But he'd just proved she had nothing to fear from an intimate connection with him. She'd conceded he'd made her feel good.

He willed her to grasp what could be grasped and take it into the future with them. It was best for their son, best for their lives, too. Surely she could see that.

'Have you had the prenuptial agreement you offered me drawn up, Ari?'

It wasn't what he wanted to hear from her. It meant that it didn't matter what he said or did, she still had a basic mistrust of how he would deal with her in the future. He could pleasure her all night but that verbal kick in the gut told him it would make no difference.

'Yes. It's in my backpack,' he said flatly.

'Have you signed it?'

'Not yet.'

'Will you do so in the morning if…if you're still feeling good with me?'

'Yes,' he said unequivocally, though hating the fact it was still necessary in her mind.

She hadn't faked her response to him. There was nothing fake about Christina Savalas and it was clear that she needed a guarantee that if there was anything fake about him, she would not lose her son by marrying him.

She reached up and gently stroked his cheek. 'I'm

sorry I can't feel more secure with you, Ari. I promise you to do my best to be a partner to you in every sense. If I fail and you end up finding someone else who suits you better, I won't deny you a fair share of Theo. I just need protection against your taking him from me.'

'I'd never do that,' he protested vehemently. 'You're his mother. He loves you.'

She heaved a deep sigh as though that claim meant little in the bigger scheme of things. 'It's impossible to know how things will turn out along the track,' she said in a fatalistic tone. 'As sincere as your commitment might be to me now, as sincere as mine is to you, it's in our minds, Ari, not our hearts, and you might not think so now, but hearts can over-rule minds. I know. It's why I never told you about Theo when I should have. My heart wouldn't let me.'

There was sadness in her eyes—the sadness of be-trayed innocence—and Ari knew he'd done that to her. Determination welled up in him to replace it with joy—joy in him and the children they would have together.

'Our marriage will be fine, Christina,' he promised her. 'I don't mind signing the prenuptial agreement. I want you to feel secure, not frightened of anything. And given more time, I hope you'll come to trust me, know-ing without a doubt that I mean you well and want you to be happy with me.'

It brought a smile back to her face. 'That would be good, Ari.' Her hand slid up and curled around his head. 'I could do with some more of feeling good.'

He laughed and kissed her.

The night was still young. They proceeded to a more

languorous love-making for a while, pleasuring each other with kisses and caresses. It delighted Ari that Christina had no inhibitions about her sexuality and no hesitation in exploring his. He hoped it would always be like this, no holding back on anything.

The commitment was made now.

Ari felt right about it—more right than he'd ever felt about anything else in his life. And he'd make it right for Christina, too. It would take more than a night to do it. It might take quite a long while. But he was now assured of all the time he would need to wipe out her doubts and win her trust. When that day came—he smiled to himself—all of life would be good.

CHAPTER FOURTEEN

TINA was determined not to regret marrying Ari Zavros but to view her time with him—regardless of what happened in the end—as an experience worth having. In any event, she would not lose Theo or any other children they might have. The signed prenuptial agreement was in her keeping.

Everyone was happy that a wedding would soon take place. The Zavros family seemed particularly pleased to welcome her into their clan and Theo was over the moon at belonging to so many more people. Plans were quickly made. Her mother had no hesitation in deciding that Athens would be the best place for her to live— much closer to her daughters—and Maximus immediately offered to find the best property for her while they dealt with winding up their lives in Australia.

Ari accompanied them back to Sydney. He organised the sale of the restaurant to the head chef and the head waiter. Tina suspected he financed the deal. Everything in their apartment was packed up by professionals— also organised by Ari—and stored in a container which would be shipped to Athens. He was a whirlwind of activity, determined on moving them out with the least amount of stress. Her mother thought he was wonderful.

Tina couldn't fault him, either. He was attentive to their needs, carried out their wishes, and to Tina's surprise, even purchased an extremely expensive three-bedroom apartment overlooking Bondi Beach.

'To Theo it's the best beach in the world,' he explained. 'He might get homesick for it. You, too, Christina. We can always take time out to come back here for a while.'

His caring for their son was so evident, so constant, it continually bolstered her decision to marry him. Theo adored him. Her reservations about his constancy where she was concerned remained in her mind but were slowly being whittled away in her heart. He was so good to her, showing consideration for whatever she wanted in every respect.

Within a month they were back on Santorini. Her mother was to be a guest in the Zavros villa until her furniture arrived for her new apartment in Athens. Maximus, of course, had found the perfect place for her. She quickly became fast friends with Ari's mother who had been organising the wedding in their absence. It was almost the end of the tourist season when most places closed down on the island. They only had a week to finalise arrangements—a week before Tina's life began as Ari's wife.

Cass had been informed of the situation via email and was delighted that everything seemed to be working out well. She insisted on buying Tina's wedding dress and kept sending photographs of glorious gowns until Tina chose one. She let Cass select her own bridesmaid dress. George was to be best man—a reversal of their previous roles.

The same church was to be used for the marriage service and the same reception centre. Both places had also been chosen for the weddings of Ari's sisters. Apparently it was customary for the Zavros family and Tina didn't raise any objection although privately she would have preferred not to be following in her sister's footsteps, being reminded of the real love Cass and George had declared for each other.

She didn't feel like a bride. She looked like one on the day. And despite the lateness of the season, the sun was shining. It made her wonder if Ari had arranged that, too, everything right for the Golden Greek. It was a weird feeling, walking down the aisle to him—more like a dream than reality. Everything had happened so fast. But her feet didn't falter and she gave him her hand at the end of the walk, accepting there was no turning back from this moment.

Her ears were acutely tuned to the tone of Ari's voice as he spoke his marriage vows. It was clear and firm, as though he meant them very seriously. Which Tina found comforting. She had to swallow hard to get her own voice working at all, and the words came out in jerky fashion which she couldn't control. But they were said. It was done. They were declared man and wife.

To Tina, the reception was a blur of happy faces congratulating her and Ari and wishing them well. Everyone from both families was there, along with Ari's close business connections and friends. Tina couldn't remember all their names. She just kept smiling, as a bride should. Ari carried off the evening with great panache and he carried her along with him—his wife.

He took her to Odessa for a honeymoon. It was a beautiful city, called The Pearl of The Black Sea, and for the first time since her future with Ari had been decided, Tina could really relax and enjoy herself. There was nothing that had to be done. Theo was undoubtedly having a great time with his doting grandparents. She was free of all responsibility. And Ari was intent on filling their days—and nights—with pleasure.

The weather was still hot and they lazed away mornings on the beach, had lunch in coffee shops or restaurants beside lovely parks, browsed around the shops that featured crafts of the region—marvellous cashmere shawls, beautifully embroidered blouses, and very different costume jewellery.

They went to a ballet performance at the incredibly opulent opera house—totally different architecture and interior decoration to the amazing hotel in Dubai but just as mind-boggling in its richness.

When she commented on this to Ari he laughed and said, 'Europe is full of such marvels, Christina, and I shall enjoy showing them to you. When we go to Paris, I'll take you to Versailles. You'll be totally stunned by it.'

He was as good as his word. In the first six months of their marriage, she accompanied him on many trips around Europe—Spain, Italy, England, France, Germany. All of them were related to business but Ari made time to play tourist with her. He was the perfect companion, so knowledgeable about everything and apparently happy to spend his free time with her.

There were business dinners they had to attend, and parties they were invited to which invariably made Tina nervous, but Ari never strayed from her side whenever they were socialising. He bought her beautiful clothes so that she always felt confident of her appearance on these occasions and he constantly told her she was beautiful, which eased her anxiety about other women.

They had decided on Athens as their home base. Tina wanted to be close to her mother and it was easier for Theo to be enrolled in the same private English-speaking school as his cousins. He accompanied them on trips which didn't interfere with his schooling but at other times he was happy to stay with family while they were away.

However, when Tina fell pregnant, as happy as she was about having a baby, the morning sickness in the first trimester was so bad she couldn't face travelling anywhere and she couldn't help fretting when Ari had to leave her behind to attend to business. Each time he returned she searched for signs that he was growing tired of her, finding her less attractive, but he always seemed pleased to be home again and eager to take her to bed.

She expected his desire for her to wane as her body lost its shape but it didn't. He displayed a continual fascination with every aspect of her pregnancy, reading up on what should be happening with the child growing inside her, lovingly caressing her lump, even talking to it in a besotted manner and grinning with delight whenever he felt a ripple of movement. He always smiled when he saw her naked, his eyes gloating over her as though she presented an incredibly beautiful image to him, pregnant with his child.

Tina reasoned that obviously having children meant a lot to Ari. He had married her because of Theo and being the mother of his children did make her uniquely special to him. If he never fell in love with anyone else, maybe their marriage would become very solid and lasting. She fiercely hoped so because she couldn't guard against the love that she hadn't wanted to feel with him.

It sat in her heart, heavy with the need to keep it hidden. Pride wouldn't let her express it. Sometimes she let herself imagine that he loved her, but he never said it. Their marriage was based on family. That had to be enough.

She was eight months pregnant and looking forward to the birth of the baby when fate took a hand in ending her happy anticipation. She'd been shopping with her mother, buying a few extra decorations for the newly furnished nursery at home; a gorgeous mobile of butterflies to hang over the cot, a music box with a carousel on top, a kaleidoscope to sit on the windowsill.

They planned to finish off their outing with a visit to a hairdressing salon which was located a few blocks away from the department store where they had purchased these items. Tina felt too tired and cumbersome to walk that far, so they took a taxi for the short trip. It was crossing an intersection when a truck hurtled across the road from the hilly street on their right, clearly out of control, its driver blaring the horn of the truck in warning, his face contorted in anguish at being unable to avoid an accident.

It was the last thing Tina saw—his face. And the last thing she thought was *the baby!* Her arms clutched the mound of the life inside her. It was the last thing she did before the impact robbed her of consciousness.

Ari had never felt so useless in his life. There was nothing he could do to fix this. He had to leave it up to the doctors—their knowledge, their skill. He was so distressed he could barely think. He sat in the hospital waiting room and *waited*.

Theo was taken care of. His parents had flown over from Santorini to collect him from school and take him back home with them. He was to be told that Mama and Papa had been called away on another trip. There was no point in upsetting him with traumatic news. When the truth had to be told—whatever it turned out to be— Ari would do it. He would be there for his son.

His sisters had wanted to rush to the hospital, giving their caring support but he'd told them not to. He didn't want their comforting gestures. He was beyond comfort. Besides, it would be a distraction from willing Christina to get through this. She had to. He couldn't bear the thought of life without her.

Cassandra was flying in from Rome to be with her mother. He didn't have to worry about Helen—just bruises, a broken arm, and concussion. Her relatives were sitting with her and she would be allowed out of hospital tomorrow. She was frantically worried about

Christina. They all were, but he didn't want to listen to any weeping and wailing. He needed to be alone with this until the doctors came back to him.

Head injuries, smashed clavicle, broken ribs, collapsed lung, ripped heart, and damage to the uterus, but the baby's heart was still beating when they'd brought Christina into the emergency ward. A drug-induced coma was apparently the best state for her to be in while undergoing treatment for her injuries and it had been deemed advisable to perform a Caesarian section. It wasn't how Christina had wanted the baby delivered but he'd been told there was no choice in these circumstances.

Their second child…

A brother or sister for Theo…

They'd been so looking forward to its birth, sharing it together. Now it felt like some abstract event…in the hands of the doctors. No mutual joy in it. A baby without a mother unless Christina survived this.

She had to, not only for their children, but for him.

She was his woman, the heart of his life, and his heart would be ripped out if she died. Just thinking about it put one hell of a pain in his chest.

One of the doctors he'd spoken to entered the waiting room, accompanied by a nurse. Ari rose to his feet, his hands instinctively clenching although there was nothing to fight except the fear gripping his stomach.

'Ah, Mr Zavros. The Caesarian went well. You're the father of a healthy baby girl.'

The announcement hit the surface of his mind but didn't engage it. 'And Christina?' he pressed.

'Your wife will be in the operating theatre for some hours yet. The baby has been taken to an intensive care ward and placed in a humidicrib. We thought…'

'Why?' Ari cut in, fear for the life of their child welling up to join his fear for Christina. 'You said she was healthy.'

'Purely a precautionary measure, Mr Zavros. She is very small, a month premature. It is best that she be monitored for a while.'

'Yes…yes…' he muttered distractedly, his mind jagging back to Christina. 'The injuries to my wife…it *is* possible that she can recover from them?'

'One cannot predict with certainty but there is a good chance, yes. The surgeons are confident of success. If there are no complications…' He shrugged. 'Your wife is young and healthy. That is in her favour.'

Please, God, let there be no complications, Ari fiercely prayed.

'If you would like to see your daughter now…?'

His daughter. Their daughter. Seeing her without Christina at his side. It felt wrong. There was a terrible hollowness in his heart. It should have been filled with excitement. And that was wrong, too. Their baby girl should be welcomed into this world, at least by her father.

'Yes… please…' he replied gruffly.

He was escorted to the maternity ward and led to where his daughter lay in a humidicrib attached to monitoring wires. She looked so little, helpless, and again Ari was assaulted by a wretched sense of powerlessness. Right now he couldn't take care of Christina or their child. He had to leave them both in the hands of others.

A smile tugged at his lips as he stared down at the shock of black hair framing the tiny face. Christina's hair. Her lips were perfectly formed, too, just like her mother's.

'Would you like to touch her?' the nurse beside him asked.

'Yes.'

She lifted the lid of the humidicrib. He reached out and gently stroked the super-soft skin of a tiny hand. It startled and delighted him when it curled tightly around one of his fingers. Her eyes opened—dark chocolate eyes—and seemed to lock onto his.

'I'm your Papa,' he told her.

Her little chest lifted and a sigh whispered from her lips as though the bond she needed was in place. She closed her eyes. The grip on his finger slowly eased.

'Be at peace, little one. I'm here for you,' Ari murmured.

But she would need her mother, too.

He needed Christina, though he wasn't sure how much that would mean to her. She had accepted him as her husband. He saw the love she openly showered on their son, but whatever was in her heart for him had always been closely guarded.

So he willed her to live for their children.

That was the stronger pull on her.

Her son and her daughter.

CHAPTER FIFTEEN

Six weeks… They'd been the longest six weeks of Ari's life. The doctors had explained it was best that Christina remain in a coma until the swelling of her brain had gone down and her injuries had healed. They had also warned him she would initially feel lost and confused when they brought her out of it and would need constant reassurance of where she was, why, and what had happened to her.

Most probably any dreams she may have had during this time would be more real to her than reality and it would require patient understanding from him to deal with her responses to the situation. Ari didn't care how much patient understanding he had to give as long as Christina came back to him. Yet as mentally prepared as he was to deal with anything, it hit him hard when she woke and stared at him without any sign of recognition.

Tears welled into her eyes.

He squeezed her hand gently and quickly said, 'It's okay, Christina. Everything's okay.'

'I lost the baby.'

'No, you didn't,' he vehemently assured her. 'We have a beautiful little baby girl. She's healthy and happy and Theo adores her. We've named her Maria—your favourite name for a girl—and she looks very like you.'

The tears didn't stop. They trickled down her cheeks.

Ari told her about the accident and the need for a Caesarian birth and how their daughter was thriving now. She kept staring at him but he didn't think she was registering anything he said. The look of heart-breaking sadness didn't leave her face. After a while she closed her eyes and slid back into sleep.

He took Theo and Maria with him on his next visit, determined to set Christina's mind at rest.

Again she woke and murmured the mournful words, 'I lost the baby.'

'No, you didn't,' he assured her. 'Look, here she is.'

He laid Maria in her arms and she stared at the baby wonderingly as he explained again about the accident and their daughter's birth. Then Theo, super-excited at having his mother finally awake from her long sleep, chattered non-stop, telling her everything about his new sister. She smiled at him and was actually smiling at the baby as her eyes closed. Ari hoped her sleep would be less fretful now.

Yet from day to day she seemed to forget what had been said and he would have to remind her. He started to worry that she might never fully recover from her head injuries. The doctors explained that it could take a while for the drugs to wash out of her system. Until she completely emerged from her dream-state, it was impossible to gauge if there was some negative side-effect that would have to be treated.

Mostly he just sat by her side and prayed for her to be whole again.

It felt like a miracle when one day she woke up and looked at him with instant recognition. 'Ari,' she said in a pleased tone.

His heart kicked with excitement, then dropped like a stone when her expression changed to the darkly grieving one that had accompanied her other awakenings. But her words were slightly different.

'I'm sorry. I lost the baby.'

'No!'

Encouraged by the certainty that she was actually talking to him this time, he explained the situation again. There was an alertness in her eyes that hadn't been there before. He was sure she was listening, taking in all the information he gave, sifting through it, understanding. A smile started to tug at her mouth.

'A daughter,' she said in a tone of pleasure. 'How lovely!'

Elation soared through him. 'She's beautiful. Just like you, Christina,' he said, smiling back.

A frown of concern puckered her brow. 'And Theo? I've been here…how long?'

'Two months. Theo is fine. Missing his Mama but happily distracted by having a baby sister. I'll bring both of them in for you to see as soon as I can.'

'Maria…' She smiled again, a look of blissful relief on her face. 'Oh, I'm so glad I didn't lose her, Ari.'

'And I'm so glad I didn't lose you,' he said fervently.

Her eyes focussed sharply on him for several moments before her gaze slid away to where her fingers started plucking at the bed-sheet. 'I guess that would have been...inconvenient for you.'

Inconvenient!

Shock rattled Ari's mind. It took him several moments to realise she had no idea how much she meant to him. He'd never told her. He reached out and enclosed the plucking fingers with his, holding them still.

'Look at me, Christina,' he quietly commanded.

She did so, but not with open windows to her soul. Her guard was up, as it had been from the day she had agreed to marry him. He had never worn it down. He should have felt grateful for this return to normality, but the need to break through it was too strong for patience in laying out what was very real to him—had been real for a long time although he hadn't recognised it until faced with losing her from his life.

'Do you remember asking me about falling in love and I told you about the American woman I'd met when I was eighteen?' he asked.

She slowly nodded.

'It was nothing but blind infatuation, Christina,' he said vehemently, his eyes burning into hers to make her believe he spoke the truth. 'I didn't love her. I didn't know her enough to love the person she was. Being with you this past year...I've learnt what it is to really love a woman. I love you.'

Her eyes widened but still they searched his warily.

'If you'd died from this accident, it would have left a hole in my life that no one else could ever fill. It wouldn't have been an inconvenience. Christina. It would have been…' He shook his head, unable to express the terrible emptiness that had loomed while he'd waited for the miracle of her return to him. 'I love you,' he repeated helplessly. 'And please, please, don't ever leave me again.'

'Leave you?' she echoed incredulously. 'I've always been afraid of you leaving me.'

'Never! Never! And after this, let me tell you, I'm going to be nervous about letting you out of my sight.'

She gave him a rueful little smile. 'That's how I felt… nervous when you were away from me. Women always look at you, Ari.'

'They don't make me feel what I do for you, Christina. You're my woman, the best in the world. Believe me.'

Tina wanted to. Somehow it was too much…waking up from the dreadful nightmare of loss and being handed a lovely dream. She lifted her free hand to rub her forehead, get her mind absolutely clear.

'My hair! It's gone!'

'It's growing back,' Ari instantly assured her. 'They had to shave it for the operation.'

Tears spurted into her eyes as she gingerly felt the ultra-short mat of hair covering her scalp. Ari had liked it long so she had let it grow after their wedding. She remembered taking the taxi to the hairdressing salon…

'My mother!'

'She's fine. Minor injuries. She was only in hospital for one day. Everything's fine, Christina. Nothing for you to worry about.'

'Who is looking after the children?'

'The housekeeper, the nanny for Maria, your mother, my mother, my sisters, your aunts…our home is like a railway station for relatives wanting to help.'

The sudden rush of fear receded, replaced by a weird feeling of jealousy that a nanny was replacing her for Maria. 'I need to go home, Ari,' she pleaded.

'As soon as the doctors permit it,' he promised.

'I need to see my children.'

He squeezed her hand. 'You rest quietly now and I'll go and get them, bring them here for you to see. Okay?'

'Yes.'

He rose from the chair beside her bed and gently kissed her forehead. 'Your hair doesn't matter, Christina,' he murmured. 'Only you getting well again matters.'

The deep caring in his voice washed through her, soothing the tumult of emotions that had erupted. Everything was all right. Ari always made perfect arrangements. And he'd said he loved her.

She didn't rest quietly. No sooner had Ari gone than doctors came, asking questions, taking her blood pressure, checking tubes and wires, removing some of them. She had questions for them, too. By the time they left she knew precisely what she had been through and how devoted her husband had been, visiting her every day, doing his best to console her whenever she'd shared her nightmare with him.

The doctors had no doubt that Ari loved her.

Tina started to believe it.

Theo came running into the hospital room, his face

lighting up with joy at seeing her awake and smiling for him. 'Mama! Mama! Can I hug you?'

She laughed and made room on the bed for him to climb up beside her. 'I want to hug you, too.' Her beautiful little son. Hers and Ari's. It was wonderful to cuddle him again.

'And here is my sister,' he declared proudly as Ari carried their baby into the room, grinning delightedly at the two of them together.

Theo quickly shuffled aside to let Ari lay the baby in her arms. Tina felt a huge welling of love as her gaze roved over her daughter, taking in the amazing perfection of her.

'Maria's got more hair than you, Mama,' Theo said, and she could laugh about it, no longer caring about the loss of her long, glossy locks.

'She has your mother's hair, and her eyes and her mouth,' Ari said, as though he was totally besotted by the likeness to her.

Tina couldn't help smiling at him. He smiled back and the words simply spilled out of the fullness of her heart. 'I love you, too, Ari.'

His eyes glowed a warm gold. He leaned over and kissed her on the mouth. 'I will thank God forever that you've come back to us, Christina,' he murmured against her lips, leaving them warm and tingling, making her feel brilliantly alive.

A new life, she thought. Not only for the baby in her arms, but for her and Ari and Theo, too.

A family bonded in love.

It was what her father had wanted for her.

No more disappointment.
She had it all.

It was summer on Santorini again and both families
had gathered in force to attend Maria's christening. The
same church, the same reception centre, but for Tina,
this was a much happier occasion than her wedding.
Although Ari's family had welcomed her into it before,
she really felt a part of it now, and she also felt much
closer to her own family, no longer having the sense of
being an outsider who had broken the rules.

It was a truly joyous celebration of life and love. The
sun shone. There were no shadows between her and Ari.
She saw desire for her simmering in his eyes all day and
her own desire for him was zinging through her blood.
No sooner was the party over and the children finally
asleep in their part of the Zavros villa, than they headed
off to their own bedroom, eager to make love. But before they did, there was one thing Tina wanted to do.

She'd put the prenuptial agreement in the top drawer
of the bedside table and she went straight to it, took it
out and handed it to Ari. 'I want you to tear this up.'

He frowned. 'I don't mind you having it, Christina.
I want you to feel secure.'

'No. It's wrong. It's part of a bad time that's gone,
Ari. If you were asking me to marry you now, I wouldn't
insist on a prenuptial agreement. I trust you. I believe
what we have is forever. It is, isn't it?'

He smiled. 'Yes, it is.'

He tore it up.

She smiled and opened her arms to him, opened her

heart to him. 'I love you. I love our family. We're going to have a brilliant life together, aren't we?'

He laughed, lifted her off her feet, twirled her around and dumped her on the bed, falling on top of her, although levering his weight up on his elbows as he grinned down at her. 'Brilliant and beautiful and bountiful, because I have you, my love.'

She reached up and touched his cheek, her eyes shining with all he made her feel.

'And I have you.'

* * * * *

Read on for a sneak preview of Carol Marinelli's
PUTTING ALICE BACK TOGETHER!

Hugh hired bikes!

You know that saying: 'It's like riding a bike, you never forget'?

I'd never learnt in the first place.

I never got past training wheels.

'You've got limited upper-body strength?' He stopped and looked at me.

I had been explaining to him as I wobbled along and tried to stay up that I really had no centre of balance. I mean *really* had no centre of balance. And when we decided, fairly quickly, that a bike ride along the Yarra perhaps, after all, wasn't the best activity (he'd kept insisting I'd be fine once I was on, that you never forget), I threw in too my other disability. I told him about my limited upper-body strength, just in case he took me to an indoor rock-climbing centre next. I'd honestly forgotten he was a doctor, and he seemed worried, like I'd had a mini-stroke in the past or had mild cerebral palsy or something.

'God, Alice, I'm sorry—you should have said. What happened?'

And then I had had to tell him that it was a self-diagnosis. 'Well, I could never get up the ropes at the gym at school.' We were pushing our bikes back. 'I can't blow-dry the back of my hair…' He started laughing.

Not like Lisa who was laughing at me—he was just laughing and so was I. We got a full refund because we'd only been on our bikes ten minutes, but I hadn't failed. If anything, we were getting on better.

And better.

We went to St Kilda to the lovely bitty shops and I found these miniature Russian dolls. They were tiny, made of tin or something, the biggest no bigger than my thumbnail. Every time we opened them, there was another tiny one, and then another, all reds and yellows and greens.

They were divine.

We were facing each other, looking down at the palm of my hand, and our heads touched.

If I put my hand up now, I can feel where our heads touched.

I remember that moment.

I remember it a lot.

Our heads connected for a second and it was alchemic; it was as if our minds kissed hello.

I just have to touch my head, just there at the very spot and I can, whenever I want to, relive that moment.

So many times I do.

'Get them.' Hugh said, and I would have, except that little bit of tin cost more than a hundred dollars and, though that usually wouldn't have stopped me, I wasn't about to have my card declined in front of him.

I put them back.

'Nope.' I gave him a smile. 'Gotta stop the impulse

spending.'

We had lunch.

Out on the pavement and I can't remember what we ate, I just remember being happy. Actually, I can remember: I had Caesar salad because it was the lowest carb thing I could find. We drank water and I *do* remember not giving it a thought.

I was just thirsty.

And happy.

He went to the loo and I chatted to a girl at the next table, just chatted away. Hugh was gone for ages and I was glad I hadn't demanded Dan from the universe, because I would have been worried about how long he was taking.

Do I go on about the universe too much? I don't know, but what I do know is that something *was* looking out for me, helping me to be my best, not to **** this up as I usually do. You see, we walked on the beach, we went for another coffee and by that time it was evening and we went home and he gave me a present.

Those Russian dolls.

I held them in my palm, and it was the nicest thing he could have done for me.

They are absolutely my favourite thing and I've just stopped to look at them now. I've just stopped to take them apart and then put them all back together again and I can still feel the wonder I felt on that day.

He was the only man who had bought something for me, I mean something truly special. Something beautiful, something thoughtful, something just for me.

© Carol Marinelli 2012

Available at millsandboon.co.uk

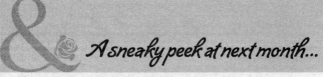

A sneaky peek at next month...

MODERN™

INTERNATIONAL AFFAIRS, SEDUCTION & PASSION GUARANTEED

My wish list for next month's titles...

In stores from 17th February 2012:

❏ Roccanti's Marriage Revenge — Lynne Graham

❏ Sheikh Without a Heart — Sandra Marton

❏ The Argentinian's Solace — Susan Stephens

❏ Girl on a Diamond Pedestal — Maisey Yates

In stores from 2nd March 2012:

❏ The Devil and Miss Jones — Kate Walker

❏ Savas's Wildcat — Anne McAllister

❏ A Wicked Persuasion — Catherine George

❏ The Theotokis Inheritance — Susanne James

❏ The Ex Who Hired Her — Kate Hardy

Available at WHSmith, Tesco, Asda, Eason, Amazon and Apple

Just can't wait?

Visit us Online

You can buy our books online a month before they hit the shops! **www.millsandboon.co.uk**

0212/01

Book of the Month

MILLS & BOON

KAREN WHIDDON

WOLF WHISPERER

nocturne

We love this book because...

Karen Whiddon's fan favourite THE PACK series continues in this powerful and enchanting paranormal romance. When a gorgeous—and dangerous—stranger shows up at Kelly's ranch, her life is never going to be the same again...

On sale 17th February

Visit us Online

Find out more at
www.millsandboon.co.uk/BOTM

0212/BOTM